I0671116

Black Dogs Unleashed: The Tenth Anniversary Anthology

Black Dog Writers of Huntington, WV

Edited by
Beverly Delidow
Jenny Grover
Carol Brodtrick

Copyright © 2008 by Black Dog Writers of Huntington, WV
Carol Brodtrick, Jennifer Cavender, Beverly Delidow, Jenny
Grover, Marie Manilla, Paul Martin, Llewellyn McKernan, Marc
Miller, S. Diane Wellman, Matthew Wolfe

Cover designed by Beverly Delidow

All rights reserved. No part of this book may be reproduced in any
form without express permission, except by a reviewer who may
quote brief passages in review.

Published by Black Dogs Paw Print Press
5 Rissa Lane
Huntington, WV 25704

Paperback first edition.

ISBN 978-0-615-25814-0

Printed in the United States

Black Dog Writers of Huntington, West Virginia
A Short History

By Marie Manilla and Matthew Wolfe

Our first meeting took place on November 1, 1998, when three local writers gathered to critique each other's prose. The group has met monthly ever since.

In the summer of 1999, we appropriated the name Black Dogs. Marie Manilla's black dog, Snickers, was making a nuisance of herself at a meeting. Llewellyn McKernan reminded us that "Black Dog" was a metaphor for depression – so appropriate since many writers struggle with that problem. We decided then to adopt the metaphor and honor Snickers at the same time.

Over the years, members have come and gone, but The Black Dogs have always had a solid core membership, with numbers ranging from 6 to 12. There have been over 20 members of the group, and two of the original three are still members today. Almost all have gone on to publish works critiqued by the group. Many have published books, won awards, and at least five have received Artist Fellowships from the West Virginia Commission on the Arts.

The Black Dogs have given six public readings. We compiled this anthology to commemorate our tenth anniversary, November 1, 2008.

The front and back covers of this book feature photos of our black dogs and honorary pack members. Front cover, clockwise from top right: Snickers, Bear, Lainey, Leah, Peigi, Jason, and Luke.
Back cover, from top: Sam and Daisy, Duchess, Blackie, and Tip.

TABLE OF CONTENTS

Black Dogs Unleashed:
The Tenth Anniversary Anthology

Jennifer Cavender is a West Virginia native and a novelist at heart, wishing to live with her characters rather than take snapshots or cross sections of their lives. She completed *Capers Island*, a novel, for her thesis while working on an MA in English Literature at Marshall University. She is currently enrolled in the Psychology doctoral program at Marshall, where she is further examining the enigma of human behavior.

A House Where All the Rooms Aren't on the Left Side

"I wish," says Stevie.

"You wish for what?" I ask.

Stevie does that. Only says parts of sentences, like he doesn't know how to finish them. His brain's so smart that I think he finishes sentences in his head, and forgets that he didn't say them out loud. Stevie has a small head. There's not much space inside for his big brain. Maybe his brain smushes the sentences before they pop out.

"Me too. I wish," says Jessie.

"You guys have to wish for something," I say.

"I wish I could play football," says Jessie.

"But, you're a girl," I say, and yank on her long, brown ponytail. Her hair feels like carpet.

"I wish I was a boy then."

Jessie doesn't know what she wants. She's two years younger than me and Stevie. She hasn't figured out what kind of person she wants to be yet, so she stitches pieces of everyone else's personalities together like a quilt.

"What do you wish for Stevie," I say again. With Stevie, you have to push him to stay on topic.

"You'll call me stupid," he says.

We're lying on an old sheet in Jessie's front yard. She's the only one who has a yard, and it's not quite flat. The yard is slanted, and we're lying with our feet up over our heads. Stevie says if we supply our brains with more oxygen, we'll get smarter. He should

1

know. He gets all A's on his report card. Even in algebra, and he's only in the seventh grade. I'm still taking boring math. The kind where all we work with is numbers. Stevie showed me some of his homework, and his math has letters. Mostly X's, but not in a multiplication kind of way, he says. They stand for the numbers.

Stevie wants to be a doctor when he grows up. I keep telling him that he'll never make it through school because of the money. Doctors have to study forever, and school's so hard that there's no way he could work and go to medical school. Maybe college, but definitely not medical school.

"Come on, Stevie," I say, poking him in the ribs. He hates it. "We won't call you stupid, will we, Jessie?"

"I wish I could know what you want," she says.

"Yeah," I say. "Why would we call you stupid? They're just wishes. I wish I could have an elephant. That's stupid. Where would I keep him? What would I feed him? But it doesn't matter. They're just wishes."

"Me too. I wish I could have an elephant."

Maybe Jessie's more like a parrot than a quilt. Quilts are quiet. Parrots have small brains, and all they do is repeat what other people say. Like they can't think for themselves.

"That cloud kind of looks like an elephant," says Stevie. He points at a puffy white cloud that looks like it has a trumpet for a nose.

"So what do you wish for already?"

I'm beginning to lose my temper. That's what Mom calls it. My temper. Once I got so mad at her, I kicked a hole in our wall. I didn't even kick it that hard. The walls in the hallway, the ones that aren't paneling, peel off in white, paper strips. I swear the walls are made out of paper.

"I wish for contradictions."

"What's that?" asks Jessie.

Jessie hasn't learned many vocabulary words yet.

"Like I wish for rain so I could sit inside and read, but I wish the sun would shine too."

"I wish it would rain, too," says Jessie.

I, too, wish for rain, but not so I can sit inside and read stupid books. I wish it would rain so my trailer would be cool. We've only got one air conditioner. We squeezed it in the living room window with some plywood. It's loud, and freezes up so much, we might as well not have one at all. But, I also wish for sun because I can't do anything when it rains except sit in my bedroom.

I have tons of stuffed animals. Mom gets me one every Christmas. I still have a big, blue stuffed rabbit from when I was two. My favorite is my Holly Hobby pillow. It's as long as I am tall. Only Holly Hobby is prettier than me. I have freckles like Holly Hobby, but I have way more. They're all over my face and my arms. They're not cute.

"I don't have to wish for sun, because it's already out," says Jessie in a rare moment of clarity. That's what my mom says when I say something really smart. A rare moment of clarity.

"I wish it would snow so we could build a snowman," says Stevie.

I like snowmen. I like how the orange carrot nose looks against the white snow.

"I don't wish for winter," I say. I hate cold. Mostly, I hate sitting inside my trailer all the time. Like when it rains, I can sit in my room, or sit in the living room and watch TV. Nothing's ever on. Mom doesn't want to spend money on cable. It's embarrassing.

"I wish I lived in a place where all the rooms weren't on the left side," I say.

"Me too," says Jessie.

"What difference does it make which side the rooms are on?" says Stevie.

"It would make giving directions a whole lot more fun," I say. "Go down the hallway, and it's the second door on the right. I want a bedroom on the right."

"Not like it's hard to give directions. All you have to do is open doors until you find the right one," says Stevie.

"See, the right one," I say. "Does that mean a bedroom on the left is incorrect?"

I'm amazed at my rare moment of clarity. So's Stevie. He takes a deep breath, like an old person sighing, and cracks his knuckles.

"I thought cracking your knuckles is bad," I say.

"That's a superstition," he says.

3

Jessie cracks her knuckles.

"I wish," she says. "I wish I lived in a house."

Stevie and I are both quiet. We're both thinking the same thing, but if we say the words out loud, our wishes will be real.

"Do you see the ladybug?" asks Stevie.

For a minute, I think he's talking about a real ladybug. I look on his left arm. Then I sit up so I can see his shirt. Sometimes, when we lie on the sheet in the yard, ladybugs land on our clothes. Like we're flowers.

He points to the sky.

"Where?" I ask.

"Next to the big one that used to be an elephant."

It's weird how clouds do that. Drift in and out together to make new shapes.

"I wish I could see the ladybug," says Jessie.

"I see a slicky slide," I say. "See how it goes down into the pool?"

A wall of clouds looks a little like a swimming pool. It's hot. I wish I could jump in a pool right now. Or maybe even hook up the water hose. Mom says water's too expensive. She'll take me and my friends swimming this weekend. City pools are free. Crowded, but free.

"I wish I could go down a slicky slide into a pool."

"I wish I was 18 and could move," says Stevie.

He says it real soft, almost like a whisper, but quieter.

"Uh-huh," I say.

All three of us are thinking the same thing.

Memories of Tomorrow

When my brother Andy went away to college, he left me his fishing pole, a well-worn copy of the *Wind in the Willows*, and a stack of Playboys. He also left me a white, ceramic chicken filled with pennies and a threadbare set of Peanuts sheets.

He didn't really leave them to me so much as I stole them in dribs and drabs. I think of stealing his things as his apology for deforming my foot. Fraternal twins, we shared a room inside Mom. Andy, at birth, weighed eight pounds and two ounces. I weighed five pounds and four ounces. Healthy enough, but small. I looked like a puppy that hadn't grown into her paws.

As a fetus, I had to make do by wedging my right foot against my bottom and the inside of Mom's uterus. I popped out into the world with my right foot tucked under. Mom said she exercised my foot by holding it straight when I was a baby. Later, she bought me a special shoe, but no matter what orthopedic device the doctors tried, I continued to walk on the edge of my right foot. The doctors finally admitted there must be something wrong with my tendons. Surgery might fix them. I don't believe in possibilities, though. To me, maybes and mights are just other words for no.

Andy drained all sense of optimism away from me in the womb. Later, when he walked out the door to begin his new life, he left his sense of optimism to Mom. She's taken that optimism and created memories of tomorrow.

She Photoshopped pictures of Andy. She took his high school prom picture and digitally aged him. Added a couple of lines around his eyes, and a mustache and beard. She even added a woman in a bridal gown. She printed it out with the caption. "Wanted you to have Andy's wedding picture." She sent it to me. I tucked the frame in my sock drawer. When I pull out a tank or a pair of ankle socks, I can see different parts of Andy – a smile, his amber-tinted eyes, the cuff of his sleeve. Obscured by my undergarments, the picture looks almost real.

The point, Mom was trying to make, is that we don't have pictures from Andy's wedding. We couldn't possibly have pictures. He could be dead. He could be alive. He could be living in

Altoona, Pennsylvania, with a wife and 2.2 kids. The point Mom so insanely makes is that we don't know. There is hope in ignorance, fragility in memories not yet formed.

"Someday, Dani," Mom said as she positioned Andy's wedding photo on the mantelpiece. "Someday, we'll know why Andy left us. Someday, he'll bring his wife home to meet us."

Andy's been gone for seven years – two at college and five after that. He went to WVU, a school in the mountains of West Virginia. A gray smell of dirt and soot smothers the town. It's always cold and rainy there. Andy didn't leave me his optimistic sense of perception.

Andy sees Morgantown differently, or at least he did when I knew him. He sees the green in things. Trees. Grass. Coopers Rock. Cheat Lake. All the natural places. He majored in landscape architecture. He never finished.

Mom pretended like he did. She printed a diploma and framed it. Andy graduated *magna cum laude*. She has his cap and gown hanging in the closet. She frames pictures of beautifully landscaped yards from *Better Homes and Gardens*. She claims they're Andy's best work. She hung a blue ribbon over the one with terraced steps and a fish pond.

Andy tried to leave me his sense of adventure. The summer after his sophomore year, he took a trip across the United States. He sent me postcards from places like Seneca Rocks, the New River Gorge, Yosemite, the Painted Desert. He wrote in small, pointy block letters. I have fragments of memories. If I piece them together, I can make a memory quilt. "Had the best Gatorade from the Circle K. Blue-purple almost black." "Ran out of gas. Guy in a two-gallon hat saved me." "Don't care what they say. Dry heat is still heat. Off to the Grand Canyon tomorrow." After that, nothing.

Mom's made her own memory quilt, excising the moth-eaten pieces. She never mentions the private detective we hired to find Andy, the missing person reports, the newspaper ads, the ringing telephone pregnant with dread and expectation. She doesn't wonder if Andy's coming home. She wonders when.

Every Christmas, we buy Andy presents. Is it insane of me to wish him home? To think that one day he will walk through the door? I don't pretend that he opens his presents. Mom does. She

Photoshops Andy's face onto our holiday pictures. She pastes his head, short blond hair from high school, onto my body holding his new sweater. She crops out my toothpick slim legs, my deformed foot.

Why do I play her game? When I see the photos, I imagine he's really there. Complaining about the turtleneck, how the neck is too confining for his body. Because if not, I'm afraid I'll forget him. Memories are like spun sugar. Crystalline in texture. Fleeting as a moonbeam.

S. Diane Wellman has an M.A. in English from Marshall University. She lives in Huntington.

Vignettes from a Young Girl's Life

The Beginning

It's 1961 and I'm three years old when my mother walks out on my father. Veiled legend has it that he says he's going for a gallon of milk and doesn't return for days. Sometimes he comes home bleary-eyed with pockets full of money from a hot poker game; other times he comes back with nothing, not even the milk. Mamaw, my maternal grandmother, hates him and swears that once Mom leaves him he'll never cross the bridge to her house again, not to see Mom, not to see me, not to see the baby in Mom's stomach once it's born, not for anything. I wait on Mamaw's front porch all the same.

My first memory is of cigarettes and jovial men who chat as my father deftly throws cards in a circle. A big woman with an apron and button earrings comes and goes with refreshments. *Are you that little girl on the Sunbeam bread package?* she asks. I have a special seat in a tall chest of drawers that stands behind the card table. The top drawer is pulled halfway out and stuffed with a white bed pillow. I eat raisins one at a time from a little green box and feel like a queen on a cloud.

Years later I find a rare photograph of him, one that shows his face instead of a jagged hole created by Mom's scissors. He's walking toward a small plane, looking back over his shoulder into the camera, smiling, happy.

I understand why Mom left him, why she chose a good man for her next husband, for my and my unborn brother's next father. It's Mamaw I'm upset with, standing at the foot of the bridge, hands on her thick waist, true to her word.

Religion

I'm asleep in bed when Mom and Dad return from church. My stepsister, Clarissa, is asleep beside me. She's fifteen and allowed to watch my brother, our baby sister, and me. She's beautiful, not too friendly, and usually causing some kind of trouble. Mom strokes my hair till I wake up.

"I've got something to tell you," she says, waking Clarissa, too. This is highly unusual behavior. I think the house is on fire.

"I've been saved."

"From what?" I say, throwing back the covers.

"Your Dad and I got saved at church tonight. It means we let Jesus into our hearts. Now He'll protect us and take us to Heaven when we die. It's a wonderful thing to be saved." Clarissa flounces back over on her side without a word and pulls the covers over her ears. "Go back to sleep now. I just wanted you to know."

I soon realize that being saved means going to church three times a week, twice on Sundays, and every single night when a revival or Vacation Bible School takes place. Mom plays piano for the church and is there every time the doors open. Worse still, the church is thirty miles away in Prichard, where my family has gone since God himself invented religion. Luckily, my cousin, Ann, one year older and wiser than me, is forced to go too, since her dad, Uncle Bill, is a preacher, and her mom, Aunt Bounce, sings alto in the choir. Lucky for Ann she only has to travel to the mouth of her hollow.

Unlike Moses in the Wilderness, Ann and I come to church prepared: paper, pencils, snacks, homework. In an effort to communicate quietly, we learn sign language from a deaf mute card. Occasionally someone in the congregation requests we sing a song. Ann almost always sings "I'm Building a Bridge." I have a larger repertoire since Mom practices hymns at home and travels locally from church to church with The Melodious Gospel Quartet. They've made three LP's and use our living room for rehearsals.

Being pubescent girls, twelve and thirteen, on the verge of womanhood and sin, Ann and I are targets for redemption. It's Wednesday night at Grace Methodist and the service is coming to an end. Mom quietly plays "Just As I Am" while Preacher Bias, old,

9

skinny, and turtle faced, walks up and down the center aisle, Bible in hand, making eye contact with the unsaved: Ann and me. *Are you ready to die? If Gabriel's trumpet sounds tonight, are you ready to go? Have you accepted Jesus Christ as your personal savior? Let me tell you, friends, if you have, there's a crown awaiting you in Glory, where streets are paved of gold and pain shall be no more. But if you have not accepted the Lord Jesus Christ, who gave his only begotten son that whosoever believeth in Him shall not perish but have everlasting life, if He is not in your heart, sinner, you will burn in Hell for eternity!* Ann hands me her can of shoestring potatoes and walks down the aisle.

As we drive home, my brother sleeps beside me in the back seat and my sister sleeps in the front. We've not passed a car for miles. Mom quietly looks out the window at the dark passing hillside, and Dad listens to a Cincinnati Reds ballgame. Pete Rose hits a homerun. I bet I'm the only sinner left in that church.

The following Sunday night after determining that, indeed, I am the only sinner at Grace Methodist, I wait for the invocation then timidly walk down the aisle to redemption. Dad stands at the altar with me, his arm around my shoulders, while Mom plays "Amazing Grace." I cry, not sure if my emotions are from the spirit of the Lord, or because I feel like I've just given up my freedom. Immediately afterwards, Ann and I decide to get baptized together.

It's a beautiful Sunday afternoon; the hills are emerald green. Ann and I stand on either side of Uncle Bill, holding his hand, and wade fully clothed into Gragston Creek. Uncle Bill's tie floats. The water is warm and brown. There's a footbridge above us to the right. People stand on the bridge and around the shore and sing "Shall We Gather at the River." Uncle Bill says, *I baptize you in the name of the Father, the Son, and the Holy Spirit,* and he pushes us backwards. I glance at Ann, who unceremoniously takes a deep breath, puffs out her cheeks and holds her nose. No way, I think, and fall back gracefully, hand to my side. The water washes over me, shoots straight up my nose and down the back of my throat. I panic. I'm choking when Uncle Bill pulls us from the water, but I'll choke to death before I let on in front of this crowd. Somehow I hear old Mrs. Cooksey, 102, call out from the bridge, "Bless 'em good, Lord!" I bury my face in Uncle Bill's side as though I'm crying, and blow hard on his white dress shirt until I feel murky water run from my nose. I cough and finally breathe as *Amens!* and *Hallelujahs!* fill the air. Uncle Bill squeezes Ann and me to him and kisses our foreheads. The singing begins again as we wade to the shore.

Dreamland

... Mississippi moon won't you keep on shining on me, keep on shinin' your light, gonna make everything, pretty Momma gonna make everything alright ...

The Doobie Brothers sing through the clubhouse speakers of Dreamland Swimming Pool. It's a hot July afternoon and I've just swum to the big float, a round, aqua island of concrete that sits like an oasis in the deep end of the pool. I sit down and stretch my tanned legs in front of me. Beads of water roll off my oily skin. I smell like coconut and chlorine. I face the clubhouse, an art deco, turquoise and white palace that spans the length of the pool and serves as the grand entrance. The back opens up into this paradise of blue water. You can walk down the back steps and straight into the pool. It's supposed to be the ninth largest swimming pool in America, and I believe it. I wonder how it could be that I've never been on the third floor of the clubhouse where dances and parties are held and where my mom and father used to court. I like to imagine Mom up there all dressed up, my father twirling her around the dance floor. She plays piano for the church now, and the closest she gets to dancing is tapping her foot to the Singing LeFevres Gospel Quartet. Divorce followed by religion will do that to you.

I have a rare black and white Dreamland photograph of me as a baby being held by my father on the ladder of the little slide. I'm laughing my head off. I turn my gaze to the baby pool, a football field's length away, and see that very same slide. I try to remember him holding me, climbing the ladder, looking into Mom's camera, but I can't recall a thing.

I've worn my two-piece today, and every time I dive into the water my bottoms go down to my ankles. I can barely get them up before running out of air. I wish I could hold my breath longer, like Brenda Connard, who can swim underwater from the little dive, past the big float, to the lifeguard chair on the other side of the pool, turn around, and make it back to the big float without coming up once. It's unbelievable. Her breaststroke is the smoothest I've ever seen; she half glides, half flies over the water. I can't even make it from the little dive to the float underwater, and I think I'm going to die when I'm down deep and can't get to the top fast enough.

From where I sit I can see my little brother, Mark, in line at the little dive. We've got a summer pass to the pool; almost everyone does. Mom drops us off in the morning then picks us up in the late afternoon. She gives us money for lunch at the concession stand, which has the best corn dogs and shaved ice Cokes around. I watch the diving board until it's Mark's turn. He goes to the end of the board and jumps once, twice, gets the spring up, then curls into a ball for a flip. He almost makes it but can't get his legs out in time. Not enough spring.

Time to Turn, So You Won't Burn – W-K-E-E

My two friends, Sandy and Theresa, climb the ladder to the high dive. Sandy has the best tan at the pool; she's almost black. Her silver bikini, long jet-black hair and perfect body go with her perfect tan. She gets to the end of the board and looks down.

"Hey, Sandy!" I call from the float. She spots me, and we wave. Sandy's been giving me diving lessons. She dives with her fists balled up because she says it helps break the water and keeps your head from getting smacked. So I've been diving with my fists closed, too. I've actually gotten used to it, and now when I try to dive with my hands open it feels unnatural and makes me lose my balance. I like to dive, but I've only done so off the floats or the sides of the pool. I like to practice different angles; my favorite is diving straight down. I'd love to dive off the high dive, but I'm afraid I'd belly flop and kill myself, or lose my bottoms entirely. I jumped off once and felt like a fool. I watch Sandy spring out into space, graceful and fearless as a bird. She does a jack-knife in slow motion, touches her toes with her fists then straightens out her tanned body and dives straight down. Hardly a splash. She swims underwater till she reaches the float and comes up beside me, her blue eye shadow sparkling on her dark skin. She holds on to the side of the float and turns to the diving board. We both wave at Theresa who is wearing a new white one-piece with a matching headband that holds her long brown hair in an I Dream of Jeannie ponytail. She does a perfect flip, arms and ponytail straight above her head, pointed toes breaking the water.

Sandy, Theresa, and Brenda Connard are varsity cheerleaders. I didn't make varsity because I'm not a gymnast, which is what cheerleading has turned into in the eleventh grade of 1975 – a gymnastics competition. I was a cheerleader in junior high, and last year I was captain of the "B" team. I tried out for varsity, practicing front flip handsprings till I knocked the breath out of myself. I finally learned how to do it, but when I got to tryouts everybody was flipping backwards, too. Team spirit and a good split are no longer enough. It's the marching band for me.

...Raindrops keep falling on my head, but that doesn't mean my eyes will soon be turning red, cryin's not for me, I'm never gonna stop the rain by complaining, because I'm free, nothing's worryin' me.

My secret heartthrob, Dale Persimmon, emerges from the water like a prized fish. He hoists himself onto the float, not bothering with the ladder, and stands over me dripping water from his red trunks. I suck in my gut and act outraged. He sits down beside me and stretches out his lean hairy legs.

"I didn't know you were here," I lie.

"I've been playing basketball." There's a basketball court behind our blanket area and a tennis court behind the concession stand. Dale is quarterback of the football team, number 21. Even wearing shoulder pads he looks thin, but he's fast and graceful and I've had a crush on him for over a year. Unfortunately, he's dating Brenda Connard, who sees us together from the other side of the pool. I watch her dive in and glide over the blue surface faster than a water snake.

"When does football practice start?" I ask.

"Next week. I guess you won't be cheering for me this year, huh? Sorry you didn't make the team." He sounds so genuine I'm not even upset.

"I'll cheer you on from the sidelines."

He smiles his Pepsodent smile. Brenda reaches the float and sits down beside him. "Hi, Brenda," I say, getting up.

Sandy and Theresa head back to the high dive, and my brother is on the little dive again. This time he jumps on the board till it rattles, curls up and flips. A perfect landing.

I dive in the water and catch up with him. "Nice flip, Mark."

"Thanks, Sissy." We swim to the ladder together.

"Do you think Brenda Connard is pretty?" Mark may be my little brother, but he's cute and he's in the ninth grade, and that's high school.

"She's okay, but nothing like *her*," he says, pointing to Sandy, who flies off the high dive and sails through the air like a trapeze artist.

"I wish I could do that."

"You can dive. That's just a little higher."

I look back at the float and see Brenda scowling at Dale, who's lost his Pepsodent smile. Sandy emerges triumphant from the water. Something comes over me like a spell.

"Wait here. I'm going to do it. If I belly flop I want you to pull me out, but don't let anybody see you."

"Just stiffen out and go at an angle."

Instead of climbing the ladder to get out of the pool, I swim to the opposite corner and get out by the high dive. Sandy is on the float with Dale and Brenda and sees me climb into orbit. She yells and gives me the thumbs up.

When I get to the top it's higher than I remember. I get dizzy walking out on the board; it feels like a tightrope, or a plank. I look behind me and see a line of people waiting to jump. I'm eye level with the third floor balcony of the clubhouse. I imagine Mom in her dancing dress, her future full of possibilities. In the distance the baby pool sparkles like diamonds. And suddenly, I remember. My father's arm is tight around my waist as we climb the steps of the slide and turn to face my mother's camera. Exhilarated by the height, I laugh and clutch a curl of my father's hair. "Don't be afraid," he says. "I've got you." Through space I hear Theresa call my name. I put my toes on the edge of the board, draw my hands into a fist, and plunge headfirst down an invisible angle. The water comes up to meet me, and it takes forever. My body is straight and my legs are together when my head hits the water. It feels like my skull has been hit with a ball bat. The fist theory does not work twenty feet up. I dive so far down that my hands touch the smooth bottom of the nine-foot pool. My bathing suit wraps itself around my ankles, but for once I take my good sweet time underwater and pull it back up. I push off the bottom with my feet and begin my victorious ascent, seeing the sunlight breaking through the water, four feet, three feet, two feet below the surface.

When I finally breathe air, I hear my brother say, "Way to go, Sis!" I see Dale and Sandy and Theresa cheering me on from the float. Brenda has disappeared.

As I walk back to my blanket I realize that for one moment, while standing on the high dive, I glimpsed the world for what it is: a series of snapshots. Freeze frames capture the moment and become a reference to what happened before and what happens after. My father let go of me; my mother did not. I dry off in the July sun feeling myself ripen with knowledge and age.

Marie Manilla is a founding member of the Black Dog Writers and she hosted their very first meeting in 1998. A graduate of the Iowa Writers' Workshop, her novel *Shrapnel* won the 2008 Fred Bonnie Award and will be published in spring 2009. Marie's work has appeared in *The Chicago Tribune* as a Nelson Algren finalist. She received the Lawrence Foundation Award for best story to appear in *Prairie Schooner*. Other pieces have been published in *Calyx Journal, Mississippi Review, ViêtNow, The Long Story, Yemassee Review, Timber Creek Review, Toyon, Hamilton Stone Review*, and others.

Trace Fossils

Margo squats in the penalty box lacing three-week-old ice skates, still stiff and white, no scuff marks – yet. Her classmates are already out there, tired from full days of tending children, or working, or gardening, their varicosed legs wobbly, arms flailing as they circle their instructor like a gaggle of fledglings. Mrs. Chambers stands erect and still, ceramic coffee mug in her assured, mittened hands. Margo imagines what her teacher must have looked like as a semi-pro: fifty pounds lighter, body squeezed into a tiny Lycra dress, sequins sparkling as she whooshed and spun, etching little figure eights in the ice.

What the hell are we doing here? Margo wonders about Mrs. Chambers, her classmates, herself. Men and women, middle-aged and older, trying to regain youthful grace, looking anything but lissome on the unforgiving ice. Then she hears the familiar clack-clack-clack and remembers her reason as her fifteen-year-old daughter races toward her, padded and helmeted for hockey practice at the other end of the rink. Margo braces herself as Becca nears and turns sideways, deftly jamming her blades into the ice, coating her mother in a snowy spray. Becca's father taught her that move.

"Hey!" Margo howls, shaking ice crystals from her kinky new perm that still smells like ammonia.

Becca laughs and scurries away, russet ponytail bouncing against her black jersey.

Margo stands and centers herself on thin blades before stepping onto the ice. She pulls herself along the railing hand-over-hand to join her class, pausing briefly before letting go, more walking than skating as she clatters toward the cluster of neophytes, trying not to look at frozen blood drops spattering the ice from men's hockey, her husband Carl's old league. Such a rough sport, she knows, glancing down rink to find Becca, but all the girls look the same in their face masks and baggy hockey pants.

Be careful, she prays, the same prayer she offered twenty years ago for Carl when she sat on the bleachers back in West Virginia watching him deflect pucks, sticks, and punches. Margo hated the game, shredded tissues and wax soda cups until the last buzzer sounded and he skated off, safe.

Today Mrs. Chambers teaches them to skate backward. *Quite ambitious*, Margo thinks, since they barely inch forward. She worries about the Spieglemans, a retired couple in their 70s, especially Mrs. Spiegleman, with her curved back and brittle bones. But husband and wife grasp each other's forearms and he pushes while she coasts in reverse. Her face is fearful at first, but Margo hears him chanting: "I've got you, dear. Don't worry." His wife's lips pull back in a grin as he steers her in ever-widening circles.

After practice Margo waits by the concession stand for her daughter, and there she is, hair wet, untied shoelaces dragging as she marches from the showers with her duffle bag and taped-up stick. Margo inhales when she nears, always expecting the same pungent reek Carl's bag emitted after a game, but Becca's is all baby powder and strawberry shampoo.

At home, Becca drops her equipment in the den, plops on the couch, and turns on the TV.

"Hang your stuff in the garage," Margo says.

"I will," Becca says, but she finds MTV and cranks the volume.

"Now," Margo says, and remarkably, Becca does, though her mouth presses into a grimace.

Margo wonders if this cooperation will last, or if her daughter will pull inward again into that mopey child who slunk from her room one morning after she turned twelve. Her grades plummeted. Her friends vanished. Her vocabulary reduced to growls and grunts, a garbled dialect that lasted for nearly two years.

Remarkably, hockey lured Becca from the gloom. It was Carl's idea. He brought home a flier from the rink about a new girls' league.

"Absolutely not," Margo said.

That was all Becca needed to decide that hockey could be her salvation. "You never let me do anything," she yelled, stomping toward her room.

"I'll take you," Carl said, stopping his daughter's retreat.

"You will?" Becca said, offering a smile they hadn't seen in months.

The smile softened Margo's resolve. "I guess it's okay."

And it was. Carl fitted his daughter with black hockey skates, shoulder pads, and gloves. Even took her to the rink on Sundays, his only day off, to teach her his favorite moves.

Margo drops her skates by the couch. The answering machine blinks at her. Three messages. The first one is her mother calling from Wheeling. *Just checking in,* she says. *Call me.* The second one crackles and Margo bites her tongue when a soft drawl pleads: *Margo, it's me. Could we just talk? I only want to –* Margo doesn't want to hear, doesn't want Becca to hear, so she punches buttons until it stops. "Shit," Margo says. "Shit-shit-shit." She hits erase and loses all three messages. "God," she says, fingers trembling, pulse throbbing in her ears as she wonders how Jeremy could call here, what he could possibly need. But she knows. He needs closure. Something more than the flat: *I can't see you anymore.* But how can she give him more than that? It's only been seven months since Carl, not quite seven months since she found him at two in the morning slumped over in his recliner, reading glasses cock-eyed on his face, a book about sailing wide open on his lap. She remembers thinking, when she realized he was dead, that she didn't know he liked sailing.

That was also the moment when someone, something, pressed an invisible weight on her head, her neck, pushing her into the ground, making her temples throb, shooting searing pain through her eyes, her brain, making it difficult to inch one foot in front of the other. She still struggles under that weight. God's chastening thumb.

"Any messages for me?" Becca calls on her way to her room.

"What?"

"The answering machine. Anything for me?"

"No," Margo says, hitting delete once more to make sure.

Margo closes her bedroom door and leans back against it. "I'm sorry," she whispers to the ceiling, to Carl, hoping he isn't hovering up there to witness, hoping he didn't know, will never know about her affair. "I was so stupid," she says, lifting his picture from the dresser. She remembers aiming the camera, telling him to hold still. He hated holding still, hated posing for pictures, for videos. But he did it for her. He put this quarter-million dollar roof over her head by working fourteen-hour days. And bought so much insurance that Becca can pick any college. Margo won't have to work a day in her life. Not that she worked outside the home since their marriage, though there were days, weeks, when she stood at the kitchen counter sealing leftovers into Tupperware, wondering what it would be like to have her own pay check, her own reason to shower and dress in the morning besides this.

"I'm sorry," she whispers again, and the tears come, as they always do when she thinks about her husband's generosity. Of how he provided her with everything. Every material thing. His selfless devotion. And isn't that how she met Jeremy, on men's hockey league night – Carl's only diversion that left him feeling guilty for leaving Margo all by herself – again? "Take a self-defense class," he had said. "Join a book club. Finish your degree. Get out of the house."

So she did. Dammit. Met Jeremy in the fluorescent minerals exhibit at the museum. She was leaning forward in the dim room, hands on her knees, admiring a hunk of adamite glowing lime green under the ultraviolet light. She stood there for ten minutes, twenty, captivated by the rosette cluster, the calcite crystals scattered over it here and there. She hogged the view so that other visitors could only get a sideways glimpse. But not Jeremy, who leaned in close, practically nudging her out of the way.

"It's my favorite, too," he said. "Though they have another brilliant calcite with hematite in the corner."

He pointed and Margo followed his finger, then him, as he led her to the display. They bent forward together, shoulders nearly touching, and he was right. It was truly magnificent. A fist-sized clump with nubby projections, blunt icicles poking out this way and that. A soft blue-white light emanated from within. She wanted to tell this man, this stranger, that she had a much smaller specimen at home tucked in a box at the back of her bedroom closet along with her UV light.

But she didn't. Instead she looked at her reflection in the glass case. Her hair, three feet of tawny waves covering her shoulders like a cape. And beside her, this man, younger than her, she thought, but with a kind, kind face, who loved rocks the way Carl once did.

Her husband used to have such a passion for them. It's what led him to geology. Rocks and fossils. And to his job in Houston. She remembers their first cramped apartment downtown. If they stood on the toilet they could glimpse the skyline. They took walks after dark, a canopy of live oak branches above them, cracked sidewalks below them, concrete pushed up by gnarled roots. At home, they pored over living room shelves devoted to trilobites, ammonites, brachiopods, and slabs of rock with ghosts of ferns, fish, and bird wings. They set up their own UV light and for Christmas and birthdays surprised each other with nuggets of powellite, scheelite, argonite, philogopite. At night, they turned on the UV and watched the rocks glow, marveling at the intense oranges, greens, and yellows. They lay on the floor, side by side, holding the minerals in their hands, painting fluorescent swirls and circles in the blackness. The minerals still glowed after Carl switched off the UV. He and Margo held them as the light faded, and faded, and finally disappeared altogether.

At the museum, when Margo stood, her hair caught on Jeremy's sleeve buttons.

"I'm sorry," she said, trying to untwine it, fingers shaking from embarrassment. "It has a mind of its own."

"It's fabulous," Jeremy said, taking over the task, slowly unwinding a strand. When he finished she wadded her hair into a thick bundle and tossed it over her shoulder.

"The eighth wonder," he said.

Margo reaches for that bundle now, that hair, but it's gone. Lopped off just last week with six strokes of her pinking sheers. She hoped that might lighten the weight, the constant load that jammed the vertebrae in her spine together, squeezing and pinching and bulging every disc, making her body a raw nerve of pain. It didn't work.

Becca yelped when she came home that night and found her mother's severed ponytail on the kitchen floor. "Mom! What did you do?"

"I don't know," Margo said, laughing. Crying. "I just had to do something."

Becca made her go to a salon. When Margo sat in the chair, plastic drop cloth draped over her shoulders instead of her hair, she looked in the mirror at the tired woman looking back at her, puffy eyes, deep creases around her mouth. *Who are you?* she thought as the stylist ran her fingers through Margo's brutalized mane and asked, "What would you like?"

My husband back. The last two years to do over. "I don't care," is what she said.

Margo hears, feels the pounding bass from Becca's CD player through the walls. Eight months ago she would have pummeled her daughter's door, yelled for her to turn it down. She won't utter a peep now.

Margo peels the little anklet socks from the newly formed blisters on her feet. The skates are so tight. *Serves me right,* she thinks, reveling in the pain as if it'll take a minute, a day, off her sentence. Hoping the skating lessons will reduce it, too. In West Virginia, Margo was too scared to ice skate, though it was Carl's other addiction. How sweet it would have been to join him on the frozen lake behind his parents' house. To have memories of them sashaying arm-in-arm across the ice. Memories the Spieglemans are making even now. But she wouldn't even try. Just sat on a stump with a blanket across her lap, teeth chattering, trying to read *Little Women* or *Pride and Prejudice*, words trembling on the page.

Now here she is in Texas where it snows once a decade and she's finally learning to skate. Not on a tree-lined, slick pond with snowy banks and geese flying overhead, but in a dank ice rink with mildewy bathrooms. Hating every second, but she's doing it for Becca. For Carl. Carrying on his legacy, his connection to their daughter. Trying to keep the lines wide open.

And they have remained open so far. Remarkably, after Carl's death, when the weight was so cumbrous Margo couldn't leave her bed, it was Becca who stoically accepted the neighbors' casseroles and pies, their condolences. More than once Margo, lying sleep-deprived in her room, heard Becca offering thanks and excuses: "She's just not up for company." It was Becca who served up platefuls of sliced ham, globs of potato salad, and brought them to Margo's room, sat on the edge of the bed urging her mother to take a bite. Just one.

Margo did. One. Then another. And another until she could actually stand and drag her feet across the carpet and down the hall to face piles of sympathy cards, bills, and insurance forms. So many people to notify, to thank. Only one to avoid.

But it hasn't been easy for Becca who has sucked up the tears. Held in the ache because whenever she mentions her father, her mother tunnels back into seclusion. Margo knows that this is not healthy. That her daughter must grieve. But she can't bring herself to utter Carl's name, to reach out to Becca and recall tender memories of her birth, of how Carl rocked her for hours during the colic months, papered her room with sea horses and kelp. Created an underwater world they slipped off to after dinner so he could quiz her in Math and American History. *If I were a good mother,* Margo thinks, *I would break out the scrapbooks and conjure up Carl's ghost. But I can't.* Another failure that's weighing her down.

The phone rings and Margo jumps, fumbles with the receiver on her night stand, wanting to get to it before Becca. But she drops it and cusses and when she finally holds it to her ear she hears Becca and Samantha, a school friend, railing about Biology homework.

"I got it," Becca says.

"Okay," Margo says, hanging up.

Does she have to worry about every phone call now? Every doorbell ring? Is Jeremy going to show up one day with flowers and scissors to snip the tenuous thread of closeness she and Becca now share?

Margo looks at Carl's side of the bed. The clock radio that is still set to go off at 5:30am, and she lets it. A reminder of how hard he worked. *No wonder he no longer had time for silly minerals and glow-in-the-dark games.*

Beside the clock radio is the video Carl's co-worker, Ray, gave her of his Labor Day picnic, taken three weeks before Carl's death. "I think he's on it," Ray told her. "You took some of it, didn't you?" he asked. "Yes," Margo said. She remembers taking the camera from Ray's wife, Cynthia, the real home video buff, while she attended to guests. Margo recalls panning the backyard festivities: a sack race, Coke bottle ring toss, watermelon-eating contest. But there was a bird, too, an escaped parakeet singing high up in a pine tree. Margo captured its image, too. Ray squeezed Margo's hand before releasing the tape. "I thought you should have it," he said.

At the time, Margo clutched the video to her chest and said thank you, but she hasn't had the courage to watch it. Not yet. Beside it is the book about sailing she found on Carl's lap. Margo reaches over, slides it from the table, and props it on her bent knees. She splays her fingers on the hard cover wondering if Carl's hands were there. Or there.

"You liked sailing," she says, fanning the slick pages of photographs, stopping to read captions. Don and Jennifer Graham on their Beneteau 311. Peggy Beachem and Paul Neill on their Catalina 42. All the photos are of couples smiling broadly as they prepare to head down the Eastern shore to Florida, or tack from port to port in the Caribbean. They chucked their land-lives cluttered with traffic jams, 80-hour work weeks, and car payments, for the simpler water world of boats that held all their worldly goods snugly in their bellies.

Was this your dream? Margo wonders. *To escape? Pare down your life? Were you afraid I wouldn't go with you? That I'd be as afraid of sailing as I was of skating? Is that why you never told me?*

She lets the pages fall open to the double-wide center that she's studied hundreds of times these past months: a man and woman, arms strapped around each other's waists, skin bronzed from day after day on the water. Scribbled overtop their heads in a failing pen are the words: You and me.

Why didn't you tell me?

Margo feels the familiar clench in her gut when she remembers how badly she failed him. How oblivious and innocent he was. How far apart they had grown since their days in West Virginia. But he failed her, too, by planting her in this house in the Woodlands with its community swimming pool and tennis courts and bylaws. Manicured lawns and privacy fences that made every street look like the next, and the next. And he failed her with his absence, his preoccupation with work, with finding oil and gas for billion dollar companies that always wanted more. She looks at the picture again, imagines herself and Carl standing there and hears water lapping against a bow, wind rustling palm trees and pampas grass, gulls crying. She can practically smell the briny sea spray. *We could have planned this together. Dreamt about it together. Started looking at boats, maps. It would have given us something. Like skating was for you and Becca. Like the museum was for me and –*

She won't say it. Doesn't even want to think it, to mingle his name with Carl's and Becca's. But how she yearns to conjure just one memory, to allow herself a taste of the harmony they shared. *If I do it real fast –*

And there it is, just an image, and Jeremy isn't even in it. The bedroom in his airy home in Montrose, windows on three sides open, sheers fluttering in the slight breeze. Outside, an ashe juniper sways against the house, clusters of blue berries tap the screen. *Where is Jeremy? Where am I?* Together, somewhere, on their stolen afternoons. Maybe hiking the bayou as they did so many times, looking for turtles the size of hubcaps. Squeezing each other's hands when a green shell surfaced. But back in the house, his king-size bed waits, plaid comforter spilling on the floor, sheets rumpled, imprinted with the outline of their bodies.

Stop it! The clench in Margo's gut turns to wrenching and she squeezes Carl's book until her fingertips ache. *Just stop!* she thinks, trying so hard to be true to her husband, if not before, at least after.

Becca knocks and opens the door. "Want some popcorn?"

Margo wipes her nose on her sleeve.

"You okay?" Becca asks, stepping closer.

"Yeah."

Becca sits on the edge of the bed and looks at the book. "Is that it?"

"Uh huh," Margo says. She looks at her daughter who looks so much like her father. "Did you know he liked boats?"

"No," Becca says, the same answer she's been offering for months.

Margo covers her face with her hands. "Neither did I."

Her shoulders shake and Becca leans over to massage her mother's feet. "It's okay. I miss him, too." Becca reaches for the Kleenex and pulls out three. "Here," she says, scooching over to hold them against her mother's cheek.

Margo sets the book aside and dutifully wipes her nose. "Of course you miss him. You were best buds."

"Yeah," Becca says, eyes brimming with wetness, head tipping up with a plea. "Can we watch the video?"

The weight on Margo's head doubles. "What?"

Becca nods toward the nightstand. "Dad's video. Can we watch it?"

Margo wants to say no as she has so many times, wants to wait another decade or two, but it's not fair to Becca. "Okay," she says, voice wobbly. *I deserve this pain.*

Becca snatches the tape and rushes out the door. "Come on!" she calls, feet pounding down the hall.

"O God," Margo says, but she makes herself sit up, stand, put one sore foot in front of the other until she's in the den. Becca, sitting cross-legged before the TV, has already slid the tape inside the VCR.

"Ready?" she asks.

No. "Yes." Margo sits in Carl's recliner. It's easier to sit in it than to look at it, empty.

Suddenly there's Ray and Cynthia's patio. The picture wobbles and jerks and finally focuses in on their back yard decorated with balloons, a donkey piñata hanging from a porch beam. An electric ice cream maker churning away. Ray stands by the grill, smiling. *Hold up the meat!* Cynthia calls from behind the camera. He skewers one of the 10-pound briskets sizzling on the grill. Children race around pointing squirt guns, adults cackle in clusters drinking out of yellow, plastic cups. There's Sam and Peggy Nielson. Jon and Angie Buckman. The Wilders, Tinglers, Kincaids. A black dog steals cocktail weenies from a plate someone left on the ground. *Shoo!* Cynthia says, giggling. *Go on home, now.* The shot fades, and when it restarts Rob Bowman aims a rubber ring at a line of Coke bottles.

"I took this!" Margo says. "I think this is when I had the camera." Sure enough, there are the Miller twins in a three-legged sack race. The skinny one falls, but the chubby one drags his brother across the finish line. Mel and Robby Sites try to spit watermelon seeds into a spittoon. There's Ray, banging a spoon against a saucepan as he calls Cynthia to his side for a surprise. She works her way to him, little flip of blonde hair bouncing with every step. Ray clears his throat and announces that for their 20th anniversary he's taking his wife on an Alaskan cruise. Cynthia's mouth falls open, and she must be in shock, because for five full seconds her face doesn't register. She doesn't squeal or titter, but eventually she hugs her husband and her shoulders shake from behind. Margo doesn't remember filming that. But she must have. Then she hears her own voice. *Listen,* she says on the tape. The camera swerves too fast toward the sky, a blur of brown and blue. The sound of chirping, trilling. *Where is it?* Margo says, the camera finding a spot of green and yellow in a branch. She zooms in on the parakeet madly singing, either thrilled to be out, or sending a crazed signal for its owner to come and carry it back to safety.

The camera jiggles and blurs and when the new image settles Becca cries: "Dad!"

And there he is, Carl, standing in a circle with four other men. His back to the camera. Thinning crown glaring. Arms hanging at his side, beer in one hand, cigarette in the other.

"I thought he quit smoking," Becca says, throat full of longing.

"He did," Margo whispers.

He turns, offering the camera a shy smile.

"Dad," Becca sighs. For the first time Margo sees the wetness spill from her daughter's eyes and run in rivulets down her cheeks.

All the men turn and hold up their cups in greeting. *Cheers!* one of them says. They turn back around and talk about the upcoming drill. All except Carl, who watches the camera like a skittish dog. Margo is surprised he has stood in front of it this long. Normally he would grin sheepishly and move out of sight. But he stands there, eyebrows arching as if he wants to say something. Nervously pivoting his head right and left. She tries to remember if they were arguing that day. If he's trying to make up. The strange way he looks at her, filming him, his face wanting to express something, an apology, maybe. His mouth parts slightly, then closes, and opens again as if he's trying to form words but can't find the right ones.

What is it? Margo thinks, desperate to remember the moment.

Then he says it. Or mouths it. *I love you.*

"He said he loves you," Becca says, her voice cracking before she breaks down, sobbing.

Margo wants to cry, too. Not from joy, or longing, but from guilt. She feels a burning in her throat. A flush of heat in her face. Nausea. She wants to run from this house, this subdivision, this city, and scream into the night sky: *I'm sorry! I'm sorry!* until she has no voice left.

And then she sees it.

Just a hint of color, vibrant purple with yellow triangles, in the background on the left of the screen, a woman in a garish dress about to enter, tawny cape of hair around her shoulders, but before she does Margo races to the VCR and jams her finger against the Stop button.

"Mom!" Becca yells. "Don't!"

"I can't," Margo says, chest thumping. "It's too much. We'll watch it again some other time. All right?" She tries to keep

27

her voice steady, not give anything away.

Becca's face scrunches in confusion and all she can say is, "Why?"

"It's too hard," Margo says.

"It's hard for me, too," Becca says. "Don't you know that?"

"I do," Margo says, reaching out for her daughter, but Becca bolts away and runs down the hall.

"No you don't!" she says, slamming her bedroom door.

Margo does know, just as she knows she should go after Becca to comfort her. But not now. Instead she grabs the tape and races to her room. Shuts the door. Looks at the tape in her hands. The absolving tape in her hands. Head shaking back and forth. Unbelieving. But she has to believe and she rushes to her closet and slides the door open. Starts fanning through blouses and slacks and skirts until she finds it. There. The shift dress. On a hanger she bent so it wouldn't slide off and wrinkle up on the floor. She only wore it once. That one time. And Carl said, with her hair, it really wasn't the right color. He never liked purple. And the triangles were all wrong. But what was really wrong was Carl mouthing *I love you* on tape to someone *not* wearing a garish purple dress, someone who was not Margo. Perhaps a woman with a flip of blonde hair who prefers rhythmic Caribbean waves to frozen Alaskan glaciers.

Suddenly, inexplicably, the weight that has pressed Margo down all these months is lifted in one freeing whoosh.

Margo tugs the dress from the hanger and holds it before her, fabric quaking in her hands. She starts crying, then, really bawling, and hugs the dress to her so tight it's like hugging herself, and she needs that hug, desperately, because as she stands there, something else sloughs off her head, her chest, drips off her fingers and toes and lays pooled at her feet. Margo drops the dress and steps over it and the puddle of whatever she's been living, breathing in these past months, years, decades, or however long this marriage has been over.

Then she hears it. A soft whimpering at first that grows louder and louder until it erupts into violent sobbing. Becca. Crying, at last. Filling her room with the anger and pain that's been stowed in her belly for seven months. Margo feels curious relief, like when Becca's 104° childhood fever finally broke.

At this moment, something else breaks, too. Margo walks to the closet and kneels to reach inside and slide out one box, then another, and another, taking extra care with the one marked UV. She slices through the brittle tape with her fingernail and lifts the light out, wondering if it still works after all this time. She unwinds the cord and plugs it into the socket by the floorboard, presses the switch and hears it hum as it warms and flickers to life. "Yes," she says, feeling the old energy coursing as she opens up another box, pulling out minerals she so carefully wrapped and packed all those years ago when they moved from the apartment into the first house, and the second, where they remained boxed up in her closet, waiting. She unwraps them one by one, trying to remember their names: artinite, hydromagnesite, hackmanite. She nestles them into the carpet under the UV light as she sorts and rearranges and finally finds the calcite with hematite, a tiny cousin of the one at the museum that Jeremy loved so much. That he still loves, she supposes, she hopes. She sets it under the lamp, too, then stands and crosses the room to flick off the overhead. The room darkens and she heads toward the UV, to the glowing row of minerals practically vibrating with color. She picks up the calcite and holds it between her finger and thumb, swirling it, painting the air with streaks of light.

A little moan slips through her lips and she lets it. This is real grief. Sorrow for what she lost so many years ago. A kind of sorrow she will be able to let go of, some day. But for now she will remember the nights she and Carl lay on the floor in that downtown apartment and made wishes on the glowing rocks in their hands. They dreamed and made promises that both, it seems, would break. But at the time they were naïve and lovely.

Margo wants to share this with her daughter. Before she calls to her she takes the video and turns it over and over in her hands, trying to decide what to do. Imagines yanking out the brown ribbon, foot after foot until it is just a tangle of slick film. *No. That isn't right.* Years from now Becca will want, will need, to see her father's image again, even if it's in a moment of betrayal. At least he will be there, alive. Margo drags one of the unpacked boxes toward her and pulls out a wad of crumpled newspaper. She flattens it out, places the tape squarely in the middle, and wraps it up tight, first one layer, then another, and another, so it will be safe. She puts the video in the box, packs more paper around it, and secures the flaps before tucking it deep inside her closet where her million-year-old rocks once rested. And who knows, maybe after a time it will miraculously petrify, or compress into a hard hunk of black coal that she can display with the rest of her treasures.

"Becca!" she calls out. "Becca!"

Her daughter's angry answer bursts through the wall. "What!"

"Come here!" she says. As Becca's thudding footsteps approach, Margo imagines her daughter crossing the hall, pausing just a second before opening her mother's door. And when she does, she will see darkness, then a glow and a hum and beauty she will be drawn to, and captivated by. Together they will lie on the floor, hold the rocks in their hands, and dream. Margo will tell Becca about her father's love of minerals and fossils, his legacy to her. Margo will promise to set them up in the spare room and surround them with pictures of Becca and Carl, especially the ones of them on ice, with their sticks and gloves, skating toward the camera, fighting over the puck, smiling their twin smiles. Then Margo will turn off the UV and they will etch their own glowing figure eights in the blackness until the rocks' inner brightness becomes fainter and fainter, and finally disappears, leaving only a hint, a ghost of light.

Llewellyn McKernan is a poet and children's book writer. She has lived in West Virginia longer than anywhere else on earth. She considers it her home. She has a master's degree in creative writing from Brown University. She has received eleven grants and fellowships, including a West Virginia Commission on the Arts Literary Fellowship in both poetry and fiction. She has had three poetry books published: *Short and Simple Annals*, *Many Waters*, and *Llewellyn McKernan's Greatest Hits*. She has had four books for children published: *More Songs of Gladness*, *Bird Alphabet*, *This Is The Day*, and *This Is The Night*.

The Long and The Short of It

"Life is like muddy waters that never clear," Johnny used to say and Hope agreed, for there she was on the floor without knowing much about how it happened or why. One minute she was rolling her pounds of flesh along in slippers and gown, in the dark hall, and the next the rug had jumped out from under her and she had fallen – on her side, too, with a jarring crash to her right hip bone, and her night clothes rucked up under her, and her slippers flown.

For a little while she just lay there on the cold floor, like it was what she'd planned to do all along, to break up her nightly routine. And things did look mighty strange from this perspective. The floor spread out from the edge of her eye to a rug that had scooted some distance away and was all bunched up, like a strange animal had taken refuge under it, the bathroom just beyond it a crack of light with a pane high up on one wall, through which the blue twilight shone steadily.

Hope cautiously turned on her back. (She felt a searing pain in her right thigh, then it was gone.) She raised her arms and legs feebly, to see if they were broken; pathetic little sticks they were, all stuck out above her big belly, with her working them like an overturned ant burdened with a giant crumb of some dessert. "Well, you do love your sweets, that's a fact, Hope Long," she told herself.

She'd spent her life making them and eating them, drowning them in sun brewed tea or cold homemade cider. Well, they weren't doing her any good now, it was because she was so heavy in the stomach that she couldn't raise herself to a sitting position, and try to get to her knees. For no reason she thought of her recurring dream – that she'd died and gone to heaven – and when she got to the pearly gates St. Peter told her he'd give her the keys if she'd just tell him the recipe for her famous four-layered pineapple upside-down cake, the one that dripped with rum and beads of brown sugar and little slivers of golden fruit. That one recipe she'd kept secret all her life, the name of the spice that had given it its long shelf life – the staler it got the sweeter it tasted – had never crossed her lips, not even for Johnny, whom she'd loved more than life, who had tasted her lips and all her best recipes many a time.

Now she stared at the ceiling, her pale wrinkled face aquiver, her little black eyes snapping with anger. Well, she was an old fool, that was certain. A 75-year-old woman living alone, she might have known it'd happen sooner or later. Her older sister, Grace Short, lived less than half a block away, and her being alone, too – never having married or had children – you'd think they'd both have the sense to live in one house or the other. But they'd never gotten along, and Hope reckoned after more than seven decades, they never would.

Hope was proud and people-shy. In a group her heart fluttered and jumped about so much, she shut her lips tight to keep it from leaping out, she crossed her arms and pressed down hard, she backed up against a wall and looked neither to the left or right, and lost all social graces as Grace bluntly told her to her face, "You're hopeless."

She was housebound, too, by her addiction to baking and soap operas – in both she lost all sense of time, like in those dreams where, with one balletic leap, she flew out of her own fat limbs into the Olympic body of a swimmer. Dressed in a skin-tight swimming suit, she dived like Esther Williams into one giant dish of sweets after another, her divine flesh frosted with cinnamon and sugar, smeared with cherry-filled chocolate kisses, dripping with strawberry pie filling, vanilla ice cream, etc. – food for her lover, who comes along just as she's at the peak of her eating high, and who bares his muscled chest and steely thighs and dives in after her. (His legs look suspiciously like Pierre L'Agape's, the Frenchman who appears on *The Bad And The Beautiful* weekdays from three to three-thirty on WHPM. She drowns in his soulful eyes, the whites a little yellow from too much liver bile.)

If Grace Short had had such a dream in the eighty-six years she'd already lived, why she would have died! A leather-lean woman, she had made all the right decisions in her life and knew it. Hope wondered what Grace would say when she heard about her young sister's latest escapade. She'd eavesdropped on Grace belly-aching on the phone about "her younger sister" so many times she had the harangue down pat. She could just hear her now, talking to one of her bridge buddies, her tinny voice screeching like chalk across a blackboard. *Well, you know how Hope is, she's always sick, you are what you eat, you know, and she is the spitting image of a fat stuffed roll, if I do say so myself, and then, of course, she was by herself, as usual, only one of her girls was home that day, you know she had so many kids I lost count but none hardly ever come to see her any more, not even on Christmas or Thanksgiving, and though for once Lorrie May was there, she couldn't stay, she had to get back to Conroy, her son was playing in some soccer game, it goes to show how grown-up children just don't have any love and respect for their elders nowadays, soccer being the outlandish foreign game it is, I wouldn't think she'd want her son to play anyway, and Hope had been throwing up something awful for the past few days.*

Well, I thought about spending the night with her myself, but I thought, well, it's her own fault, eating nothing but éclairs and banana pudding and sorghum sundaes, she's made her bed, now let her lie in it, if I had that chunk of junk sloshing around inside me, I wouldn't want to do anything but lie down and pass out, so I say to Hope, Hope, now I have the key to the front door so you leave the latch off the screen, so in case you need me during the night, I can get in real quick – well, Mabel, what do you suppose she goes and does? Why, she latches it tight and triple-bolts the locks, just to make sure, I guess, that I can't get in when she needs me most.

"Yes, you big dummy" – Hope gasped as she rocked onto her left side, straining to get a hand-hold on the floor, only to fall back, doubling the pain in her right thigh – "not only that the windows are sealed tight." What had she been afraid of? Breaking and entering she guessed, there hadn't been a night since Johnny died that she hadn't walked the floor, stretching out the darkness until the wee hours, always expecting to look over her shoulder and see the brute of a burglar come magically through the walls, wearing a Halloween death mask, through which she could see the hate in his eyes as he wrenched her arms behind her, twisting them tight with one monstrous hand, the other holding a knife, whose sharp point was gently, teasingly, testing the soft flesh between two ribs.

Hope shivered. The hall was cold; the floor was freezing. She always turned the heat down; her social security didn't provide enough for her to be warm all the time, her children helped when they could, but they all had huge families and small jobs and couldn't afford to give her much. She had to pinch and save at every turn. For once she was glad for all her pounds of flesh. They insulated her some from the arctic drafts roaming the house.

One hand groped tremblingly along the floorboards, trying to get a grip on something, and failing. It was a short hall, really an extended doorway between the dining room and the bath, and it had no furniture. In the bathroom window the deep purple sky turned suddenly pitch black.

Hope gave a long sigh and composed herself as best she could. "At least I have my memories," she thought, and suddenly one came back to her with absolute clarity, an especially hot day in July of '46 when she still had an hour-glass figure and Johnny a longing to possess it, and he'd come home unexpectedly from the garage they owned ("Long Service In A Short Time" was their motto) to find her raising up from the banked heat of an oven door, wearing nothing but bra and panties, sweat trickling down her back . . . She drifted off . . . shivering with pleasure as she lived again in her mind the wrenching fury with which he had grabbed her waist and spun her around, and the fiery way he kissed her, wrestling off her underclothes as she grappled with his filthy mechanic's uniform, popping off the buttons as he pulled her down, down onto the linoleum, both of them wet with sweat and anticipation, her licking the salt from his rose tattoos, his hands leaving greasy black prints all over her body. Hope shuddered . . . and abruptly came back to the present.

Goose livers and grease! She was going to be here all night. In the freezing dark. Maybe she'd have a heart attack, or die of the cold or a stroke. Angry tears filled her eyes. She tried to yell for help, but somehow the words got choked up in her throat, all that came out was a dreadful mewing. The only one who'd check on her was Grace. And that probably wouldn't be till morning.

She could just hear her now, telling Mabel the bad news, her shrill voice a scalding stream: *Well, if I called her once that morning, I called her a hundred times. I figured out real quick something was wrong. I figured I'd find her in the bed dead, like I found her so many times in my dreams, she's way younger than me you know, but she won't exercise or eat right or think positive thoughts about life, why you can't go on like that for long and not die, but believe me, I never dreamed it would happen so soon.*

The first time I called on the phone, it rang so long, I thought, why, she's in the bath, that's where she is, and can't hear me, so I tried again later. Mabel, I let that telephone ring off the hook, until finally I just took off running in my housecoat, thinking, I bet I find her dead in her bed like in my dreams. Why, I was so upset, I even forgot to bring my key or have my breakfast or anything! And then when I got there, I nearly tore out my fingernails trying to get in the screen, Hope, Hope, I called, you let me in this here minute! But there was no response, just dead silence.

So I got this ladder from her neighbor's yard, Marlin, you remember Marlin, don't you, Hope's friend, the butcher from up above Crazy Creek who came down here to live with his daughter Cherry, you know, the cripple, the one that's been wearing those artificial legs since her real ones got cut off in that automobile accident when she was young, she never married, it's a shame, she was a real good-looking woman, too, but I guess no man wants to climb in bed with a couple of stumps, does he?

Anyway, I put this ladder against the side of the house and climbed up and looked into the bathroom window. At first I couldn't see a thing, the glare was so bad, but I cupped my hands around my face and looked again, and what do you think I saw, Mabel, I saw Hope, yes, indeed, she was lying in that dark hall, I could barely

*make her out, it was so shadowy and all, at first it just looked like a
bunch of old clothes had been dumped there for the wash, but it was
her all right, after a while I could make out something that looked
like arms and a chest, and that green crepe gown she's always
parading around in and then those eyes of hers, staring up at the
ceiling like they were hypnotized. HOPE! I screamed through the
pane, GET UP AND LET ME IN! But she just kept lying there, flat
on her back, like a worn-out plastic doll, without one spring left to
wind. O, my God, I cried, what if she's dead like I dreamed, only
why is she on the floor and not in the bed like she's supposed to be?*

*So I climbed down and called the fire department, and they
came with all those new-fangled tools they got and took the screen
latch off, and jiggled the locks loose, and finally I got in, and do you
know Mabel, it was awful, it was her, just like I saw in my dreams
countless times, stone cold she was, and all shrunk up. . . Lying
there like the Angel of Death had come and plucked her soul clean
away, and that's what had been truly fat all along.*

*Poor thing, I reckon it was her time to go, I'll miss her
something awful, at least she doesn't have to suffer anymore, not but
what it was her fault, the silly woman, if only she'd lived like I do on
a diet of egg yolks and garlic and blackstrap molasses, she'd still be
sitting pretty in that foam-backed rocker of hers and watching those
dirty soaps night and day. At least I won't be having that dream
anymore about finding her dead because now I've gone and actually
done it. I tell you it used to scare me awake. I'd sit straight up in
bed, the sweat pouring off me.*

Hope heaved herself over onto her stomach, biting her
tongue from the agony in her hip, and muttered, "I won't give Grace
the satisfaction." Gathering all her strength, and stretching her arms
to their fullest extent, she dragged herself forward little by little with
her hands until she reached the dining room, gritting her teeth from
the scream of pain pressing against them. It felt like something was
making its way out of her thigh with teeth that bit down harder with
every inch she advanced across the rug to where the telephone sat on
a side table.

Once she fainted from the pain, but came to again, wet with
perspiration, dazed, not knowing where she was or what was
happening, the room full of dizzily spinning shadows, going around

and around, spiraling to some final conclusion she could not grasp
or comprehend . . . scenes from her past tunneling into the present in
bright multi-colored hues . . . John, her husband (dead for twenty
years, how she missed him) back – bright red in the Santa suit he
wore to fool the children when they were little, he stood over her,
shaking a long finger at her, "Get up, Hope," he said, "the Christmas
goose is burning." Then little Iris ran in, dressed like an angel for
the church pageant, her sequin wings sparkling with promise, her
white face lovely as a flower, but her little head bald and her body
wasted to a string like it had been after the chemotherapy that hadn't
saved her in the end from being eaten up by cancer. Now the
precious thing was laughing, eating one butter cookie after the other,
the sugar frosting falling in snow-white splendor until Hope herself
was covered in the strange dear glitter, up to her eyes, and then past,
such sweet obliteration. "Momma, come back, come back . . ." the
frail child cried . . . and John, Jr., her son, the one the Korean War
had taken from her, for one brief flashing moment, he hunkered
down, to lift her up in his arms, and stand – she enveloped by his
warm solid flesh – and he transfixed by what he saw in front of
them: a moon-colored table and on it a spread of hot steaming
dishes. A world filled to the borders with many-splendored things: a
huge forest of vinegary greens, beyond it cloud-light rolls and below
it gold fields of butter-glazed corn casseroles where pimentos posed
like tiny red birds. Whole continents of cinnamon-spiced sweet
potatoes rose, and mountains of hot pungent venison. And here and
there roast turkeys sat like hills, all trussed up with stuffing, and
coated with thick brown gravy . . . all about drifted a sea of
chocolate, milky and black and creamy with caramel, where pecan
pies floated like islands and strawberry shortcake drifted like a boat
on its own juicy red waves.

"Momma," her son said, gazing in awe at the roasted pig
with an apple stuffed in its mouth. "I think I've died and gone to
heaven."

That's when she came back down to earth with a thump, a
thud, a hard bang on her forehead where she'd pulled the telephone
down on her. But it didn't matter, nothing mattered but that she
dialed with trembling fingers the right number and listened to it ring
at the other end of the tunnel.

"Hello, hello," the voice said irritably. "Don't you know it's two o'clock in the morning . . . "

Hope, breathing heavily, gasped out unintelligible words.

"Is this an obscene phone call?" Marlin Depp said. "Because if it is, I'm hanging up."

Hope finally got out his name . . . That was about the best she could do.

"Is that you, Hope?" he yelled. "Is something wrong? Never mind . . .I'll be over there soon's I can find those keys you gave me. Yes, yes, I know how to jiggle a latch off with a fingernail file. I've done it many a time. Everything's going to be all right. Just stay where you are."

"As if I was going anywhere in my state," Hope thought, as she settled down to wait, adjusting her hip to the rhythm of a steady ache.

Matthew "Wa-ya" Wolfe, a writer and musician, recently discovered that chickens don't have belly buttons. Such is his mind. His writing has appeared in *Newsweek, Animus, Yellow Medicine Review, ABZ*, and even *Reader's Digest*. He also received the 2005 West Virginia Artist Fellowship. The story, "Ezekiel," is from his collection about mystics and mystical experiences. Waya is currently working on a "musical novel," whatever that may be, and plays "Jessica," his guitar, as often as he can.

Ezekiel

It is simple: words have power. All the power.

Words destroy and create.

Yet, it took me over fifty years to realize this one and only truth: God said, and it was so. Light and darkness. Earth and moon. Man and woman. Love and war.

God needs only to speak and it exists.

Including me.

Me and the world which exists round about our own, a world beyond all human imagination –

*****

All my life I have seen things other people didn't. Or couldn't. Or, perhaps, wouldn't. Little things: an image of a man, or woman, whom no one else saw – Synagogue walls that opened up by themselves, disappeared entirely (the rabbis and congregations continued praying as though nothing had happened) – Sand whirling in the sky when the winds were calm and quiet –

These moments were rare. Nothing to disrupt my life, really.

Oh, I would briefly worry over my sanity, but as the years wore on, I accepted them as a natural part of things.

The same was true of the occasional dream visions – dreams I'd have only to see them come true days, weeks, even years later.

Like the one I had as a child about this place I now live. I had hoped that one would never come true, but –

Of course, living in Babylon essentially against our will has been very rough. My old bones are dry and tired. Yet our forced exile to this region has heightened the number and clarity of my visions. Or maybe it's just my age. I suspect it's both.

Each day seems to bring a deeper dive into the prophetic pools of my mind where I see, hear, and feel things that are not part of this world.

It is said that Abraham had his first visions in a city not too many days from here. It is also said that Eve ate of the forbidden fruit in this same region. And I pause to wonder. Even though this is not Zion, is it not possible that the soil of this area might be sacred too? Perhaps this is a place where visions come easily.

I don't know.

After all, Abraham lived long, long ago. And it is said that God moved the trees of Eden to a mountain top in the north west.

That too is strange. So often we understand that there are bad things, omens in the north west. Madness blows in on the Northwest wind. Why would God move Paradise in that direction?

My mind once whirled to try to grasp such things, as I feared for my own sanity. But no more. I know what I see and feel.

*****

When I tell other people of my visions they laugh. They mock and threaten me. They call me crazy – but it no longer matters.

As I walk the dirt roads and watch the sun paint the desert, I know that there is another world wrapped around this one. Heaven is not above. Sheol is not below. These and other worlds exist in a perpetual state along side this one. And just as water can break a beam of light into a rainbow, the same Godly promise breaks forth in my eyes. Worlds within worlds, round about one another.

I am compelled to walk and survey the lines between these worlds. To walk first in one and then the other – for how can you merely live in one world when you've discovered there are others?

You must search for them, seek them out – even if you find yourself failing to appear normal in this world others see exclusively.

I have lost my position, my family, my security, my former way of life – not because of the exile, but because of the words that have been thrust into my mouth. I know the promise for our return to Zion – I have seen it. I have seen the temple we shall rebuild –

Yes, people call me crazy, an "old fool." They refuse to listen to my words. To heed my warnings. To acknowledge my insight.

So, I have started writing my visions down – the important ones at least. I have started writing down the things God shows me and tells me. I have begun writing them down though I doubt they will ever be read. The pages will turn to dust even as my bones do. Neither will be resurrected in this world. But I write the visions down anyway, hope against hope my words will survive. That men will consider them for a long time to come.

I write. I write about the exile, about armies of the resurrected. I write about the clouds of fire that whirl in from the north, the creatures with wings and four faces. I write about the wheels. Wheels that turn within wheels, round about. Wheels with eyes and spokes.

And the manifestation of God Himself above it all.

Jenny Grover is primarily a visual artist, a vocation she chose at age five. She began writing creatively at age 13. Her work has been published in *Wild Sweet Notes II, The Labyrinth, The Mountain Goat, The New Kent Quarterly, Luna Negra, The Dickensonian, Toast,* and *Violetmoon,* she illustrated Michael Torok's book *In Relation and Reconciliation,* and published her novel *Second Choices* in 2006. She created and edits *Tone and Groove* (www.toneandgroove.com). She attended the University of the South in Sewanee, Tennessee and Kent State University. An Alabamian, she now resides in Wayne County with her husband and cats, and likes to hobnob with rock musicians.

Immersed

As she gazes through the thick half-bubble of plexiglass, it slowly begins to thin, to irridesce. The deeper she looks, the deeper she sees, the more her eyes widen, unblinking, yet relaxed. She is very relaxed, and yet excited, her heart quiet, but her mind shimmering, like the shimmering all around her. She sees further than she should be able to, or did she just not ever realize she could? Somehow the staleness, the cold, the depleted air have dissolved. The lights in the cabin have long ceased their shuddering and closed their eyes. The window dissolves. It's not blackness before her. There are deep blues, teals, like peering through the depths of an ocean. It is an ocean. Galaxies whirl like schools of silvery fishes. Bright objects dart by her ship. She floats, suspends like a fish in cold water, adapting, becoming. . .

The radio stopped stuttering and crackling two days ago, but it is not silent here. She hears, or feels deep reverberations, vibrations, almost imperceptibly high ripples. Is this the so-called music of the spheres? She listens, absorbs, delights, no longer bound, no longer enclosed, no longer needing or fearing. Her own thoughts bounce back to her as tones, mapping the distances, the locations of objects.

She does not notice when the suited, helmeted men break open the hatch, nor the one who rips off a glove to lay cold fingertips against her neck. "I don't believe it!" he sings, now just emerging off to the side of her consciousness. "She's still alive. Barely. But still, no one should have been able to survive this long." He smothers her nose and mouth with a plastic mask and vapor infuses her lungs. She coughs, as though it is fluid. She has breathed the universe, and now oxygen is but a thin broth. As they lift her onto a stretcher, fit a space helmet over her head, she still smiles, still stares transfixed through the window she no longer perceives.

The Tired Editor

Myriam would never have thought it possible, but she had grown tired of the ocean. Tired of the hiss of the surf, the uneventful horizon, the predictable rhythms, rise and swell and ebb. Even the hues of blues and greens and silvers that had once seemed to change so dramatically over the course of a day now merged into a homogenized dullness, the sand a strand of endless fool's gold.

She drew her distracted gaze in, back under the blue-ceilinged porch and onto the stack of paperwork before her on the glass tabletop, and read a name she would rather not have seen just then, that of another woman, one who sent in reams of mostly bad poetry, but somehow managed, out of all the fat envelopes she sent to hundreds of editors, to include enough publishable pieces that she had made something of a name for herself. Myriam's mouth twisted, pen half-heartedly poised for battle, as she wondered if it were simply the "monkey with a typewriter" syndrome, if some law of probability dictated that by the sheer volume of work this woman banged out on the keys occasionally something good just happened. Suddenly Myriam could see herself cast in the role of that unlucky clinician whose job it was to ultimately reject simian subject #4,239's seemingly pristine rendering of *The Tempest* because of a "the" substituted for an "and" in the final act.

She sighed and gazed out over the impersonal sea, trying to ignore its sounds. A greyish man moved methodically up the tideline with a metal detector. Maybe she should move somewhere else, inland. But what difference would it make in the end? A rustling Midwest wheatfield, the traffic on a Northeastern corridor, the rain that knitted the Northwest together – it would all be essy sounds. All esses, and no vowels.

The Snake in the Rafters

"Look," Kate smiled wickedly, pulling two slightly crumpled cigarettes from her shirt pocket.

"Where did you get those?" Laurie asked.

"I snuck 'em out of my dad's pack. He'll never miss 'em."

"What's under your shirt?" Laurie noted a curved rectangular bulk around Kate's waist and the way she kept a hand at the hemline.

"I'll show you when we get there." She tossed back her overly long brown bangs. "Come on."

"Where? Where are we going?" Laurie fell in with Kate's long strides.

"The old church."

"You know we're not s'posed to go there. It's posted. Besides, my mom says it's dangerous."

"It's alright. I've been in it. It's cool. You'll see. Anyway, you don't have to tell her. Did you bring anything?"

Laurie pulled a cold, wet can of beer from under her oversized t-shirt, relieved for a break from the hard chill it burned into her stomach. Then she covered it again quickly.

"One? You brought one?" Kate was incredulous.

"Two woulda been too obvious. It woulda made the shelf look too emptier."

Kate shook her head and took Laurie's sweating free hand. "Come on." They walked quickly down the gravel-strewn road, glancing around to see if they were watched, then turned the corner, stomping up little clouds of red dust as they almost ran, a heavy-footed trot. Stepping over the chain strung across the weedy drive, Laurie's toe caught it, setting the No Trespassing sign swaying. They ducked around the side of the greying, flaking building, its steeple blown off by a tornado years before, and waded through the waist high grasses and weeds, tiny seeds sticking in the dew of sweat on their bare legs.

"But how do we get in?" Laurie asked. "It's all boarded up."

"There's a hole back here big enough to crawl through." Kate kicked a worm-eaten board aside, sending grey pill bugs rolling into balls on the ground, and a ragged hole yawned in the dry-rotted clapboard.

"We'll get stuck."

"We won't get stuck. I've been in before and I'm bigger than you."

"You go first."

Kate ducked in, reaching the floor with her hands, then twisting to land on her rear and pull her legs through. She stood up and brushed herself off, looking out at Laurie's hesitant expression.

"Here," Laurie handed her the can of beer, and then slowly, warily wormed through the hole, scratching her leg in the process. She wet a fingertip with her tongue and smoothed the white scrape, then stood up and looked around. Doves cooed and scratched in the rafters. Feathers, droppings, egg shells, shards of colored glass littered the spongy wood floors. Flares of light leaked around the boards tacked over the windows and doors and shone from holes in the streaky walls. Laurie shuddered as she brushed sticky spider web filaments from her arms. Turning, she saw the wreck of an altar, gouged with graffiti, spray-painted with names. Onto it, from a hole in the roof, shone a shaft of light speckled with dust and drifting down-feathers, like some remembered visitation.

Kate kicked an empty whiskey bottle out of the way and sat down near the foot of the altar, pulling the strange parcel from under her shirt. "Look," she glowed, holding up a magazine.

"Where did you get that?" Laurie's eyes widened at the scantily clad muscle man on the front.

"I found it under my sister's bed."

Laurie sat down by her friend, who was pulling the cigarettes and a plastic disposable lighter from her shirt pocket. "Oh, my God!" Laurie giggled to hide her shock at discovering that the men inside the cover wore nothing at all. She remembered uncomfortably that she was in a church, and that her mother disapproved of the expression she had just used.

Kate lit both cigarettes and handed Laurie one, taking a deep draw and snatching back the magazine. "Here, look at this one," she flipped glossy pages. "He's my dream man."

Laurie scanned the centerfold of the blond and bronze reclining man, his wide smile barely concealing the strain of flexing as many vein-corded muscles as possible. "Nah, he's too muscly."

"Too muscly? How can he be too muscly?"

"I don't much like muscle men. They don't look normal. They're not like –" She puffed and coughed smoke.

"You're not inhaling right. Look," Kate demonstrated.

Laurie tucked her straggling blond hair behind her ears and tried again, getting some of the ragged menthol smoke into her lungs, trying not to twist her nose with distaste. She drew again and felt a little dizzy.

"Like who?" Kate prodded.

"What?" Laurie popped open the beer and took a bitter, foamy sip to soothe her throat.

"He doesn't look like who?" she thumped the muscle man's washboard stomach.

"Like Tommy," Laurie tried not to blush.

"Tommy Greene?" Kate laughed. "You like him?"

"He's cute. And he likes me," she defended.

"He likes you? What makes you think so?"

"He kissed me."

"Hell, he's kissed me, too," Kate bragged, "and everybody else."

Laurie took another swallow of beer against disappointment. "But he kissed me for real."

"What do you mean 'for real'?"

"You know," she hedged, flipping idly through the magazine, still feeling flushed at the forbidden images.

"You mean he Frenched you?" Kate laughed.

Laurie nodded and took a deep, dizzying draw of smoke, not looking up.

"You and everybody else," Kate shook her head, reaching for the can of beer. "Forget about it. See somebody you like there?"

"Yeah," Laurie smiled. "I like him." She showed her friend a slender, dark-haired man with dark eyes and a quiet smile. "He has kind eyes."

Kate laughed, spitting beer. "I doubt many people looking at that would much notice his eyes."

"That's the first thing I look at," she defended.

"Well, here, take him home with you," Kate said, pulling at the page until it tore free of its binding glue.

"No, I can't. What if my mom saw it?"

"Hide it somewhere."

"No, I better not." She took a hard swallow of beer. Feeling dizzier now, she let the rest of her cigarette burn up as she lay back on the floor, looking up at the dark criss-cross of rafters and half-fallen boards that seemed to turn. At least it was cooler in here, a break from the oppressive heat outside, a damper against the loud buzz of cicadas. Here the dark recesses of the ceiling twittered, twigs fell, feathers floated down. She heard Kate flipping pages, then a screech above, and the scratching of claws on wood as half a dozen doves scattered in a loud terror of feathers.

And then she saw it, thick and twisting as it fell, its sinuous body landing flop on the altar in a puff of dust. She heard her own shriek above the birds as she scrambled to her feet, kicking the beer can over in a spray of sour foam. As she dived through the hole in the wall, Kate fast on her heels, she could still see the glint of its black bead eyes, the whip of its mottled tail.

The girls tumbled out into the glare of day, Kate dragging the magazine by its torn cover, then abandoning it in the thick grass. "That scared me shitless!" she panted in her practiced adult language.

"Me too." They stumbled, breathless, back to the road, then slowed to an easier gait. Laurie exhaled against the palm of her hand and sniffed the remnant of her breath. It smelled of smoke and beer and she crammed in a piece of grape bubblegum to cover it. "I'll never go back in there again," she vowed, chewing.

"Not unless Tommy ast you, anyway," Kate teased, punching her in the arm.

It rained that night, breaking the heat, cleansing the saturated air. Laurie lay in her bed, unable to sleep with the rumbling of thunder and trains from somewhere across the fields. She lay looking up at the peaked ceiling of her attic room, imagining the skeleton of rafters behind the plaster, and shuddered in a lightning flash as she remembered the glint of the snake's eyes. She remembered, too, the kind eyes of the dark-haired naked man whose picture now lay beer- and rain-sodden on the floor of the old church, and she wished she had brought it home with her.

Beverly Delidow is a poet, writer and nature photographer, currently supporting those habits as an Associate Professor of Biochemistry. She is five in Black Dog years. Though her work is not yet in print, she credits the Black Dogs with giving her the push to keep writing and to submit pieces for publication. She has a novel – or two – in progress. She currently resides on the side of a pleasant hill with the fur folk, including Luke and Leah, her own pack of black dogs.

Kachina

This is the hour of dreaming, but I am not awake to that realm.

I am sitting at our kitchen table. The smooth old wood feels like the hundred years of mornings it has known, softened by laughter and coffee rings and a multitude of dishtowel ablutions. A thin shaft of light comes from the clock on the stove. It will be another hour before John is up. He sleeps like our daughter does, curled to one side, sometimes smiling slightly. Awake, their hazel eyes are identical, four owl's orbs staring at me in unison.

Alyssa has always been her daddy's girl. And that's OK. It is sweeter than life to see the two of them bent over some project together, completely absorbed. They are often more like twins than father and daughter. Besides, Tiger is my sidekick. He has hung at my feet since toddler-hood, unable to resist the temptations of garden soil or the challenge of creating meals from whatever we grow. At 12, he is as skilled in the kitchen as I, and more creative. I never would have tried that thing he did with the beans. He swears he will be a chef when he is older; I'm pretty sure he is one now. He is still a boy, but it makes me weep sometimes to think what a wonderful man he will be. If I have done nothing else on this earth, I have brought my children into it. Grace enough for any one being.

My coffee has gone cool while I sit musing. I look over to see if there is enough left in the pot for a warm-up. Ginger leaps onto the counter. I start to scold her when Riley skitters across the floor on his big puppy paws. He jumps up at her; she arches her back and jumps to the top of the fridge. Riley manages to knock over a canister with a

FOOMP!

* * *

I lift my head from the desk. Battle-ax is sitting smugly atop the dictionary, looking down his nose with a feline smirk at the havoc below. He has knocked over all of my notes. Again. He starts washing the torn ears that gave him his name, back when I first took him in. He was scrawny then. Not now. It's probably good it's just the two of us; I don't know anyone else that would put up with him.

His feline sarcasm seems to make fun of the tattered wisps that cling like cotton candy in my thoughts. The familiar cluttered desktop looks foreign through the prism of the dream. The scarred fiberboard has none of the charm of the big oak table I can still feel under my fingers. The clock on the wall says it is just past 5. The ache in my neck and shoulders will be a scourge most of the day. For the moment, I ignore it and reach for a piece of paper.

It is the hour of dreaming, and I am no longer awake in that realm.

* * *

Soft. Banky soft.
Funny brudder. Want banky. Want bear. Want Mama.
Music. Hear music. See music. Pretty music. Soft. Warm.
Rainbows come from the horsy. Soft brushy back wing-things.
Horsy nose soft. I like soft.
Happy.
Sleepy.
Banky.

* * *

I open my eyes. Laser-guided daylight cuts a swath through my head. I can almost feel the floor burn under my hair. On second thought, that's my skull pounding like the bad dream I thought I was having. Guess not. Not a dream, anyway.

The guy three feet to my left wouldn't think so. If he could think anything. Boy – That's a really nasty hole.

With sufficient motivation provided, I roll away from Mr. Dead Guy and test the fragile abilities of my limbs. Arms will push upward enough to encourage the knees. Legs --- oops.

There seems to be a problem with my right ankle. My first attempt at standing ends in a rapid crumble. That hurt. There's a metal desk near the window. I scooch over to it and begin to use it to haul myself up. Then I notice the star-like hole in the glass, pointing in the general direction of the guy who is not standing up. I think the better of making myself noticeable. It is daylight, but I don't know who's out there. I don't even know where I am. From my angle, all I can see through the windows is sky and the very tip of some sort of crane.

I look around the room for clues. There are few that I can interpret. I see the desk, an empty bookshelf, Dead Guy (being dead), an overturned old style office chair, with smooth leathery upholstery, studded in brass. One file cabinet, also turned on its side. The drawers hang out. All that remains of the contents is one manila folder that has fallen open. A hand-torn newspaper clipping has fallen out of it. Onto Dead Guy. I suppose I will have to look at that eventually. But I am distracted by what I do not see. I do not see a door.

I sit with my back to the desk and contemplate. I contemplate large red shoes.

I don't know who Dead Guy is. I don't know where I am. I don't know if whoever is responsible for Dead Guy's current state has the same in mind for me. I review what I do know.

I came to Braerton on a Wednesday. It's an old mill town, full of previously bustling factories, a few of which are being remodeled into malls or condos for the tourists and business types. It's still mostly working class. I was working a lead. The why-what-where of that escapes me. Which is very weird. I realize that I do not know what kind of lead I was following. As in – I do not know if I am a beat reporter, a curious historian, a private detective, or an undercover cop.

I'm assuming I am not, as I am dressed, a clown. I don't feel very funny. Though the shoes, under other circumstances, would be quite entertaining.

I know my name. But I don't know who I am.

Sorting out this type of dilemma usually calls for a nap. I take off one big poofy shoe and use it to pillow my head. Jeez, I hate toe-socks. Gross. I hope I can . . .

* * *

It is nightfall.

The sighing and shuffling have stopped above my hiding place. I can only assume the Large Ones have finished their meal. This is good. It means I may remind them of my presence without being banished to the basement again. I slip behind the one with the low voice and engage the "cute" function. I rise to my full height, tap my forefeet against the bent leg and speak ever so sweetly, of the desecration of their ancestors' graves. This is apparently pleasing; I am rewarded with a morsel of dinner roll. I take it – nipping the end of the proffering finger without seeming to mean to. Bread, indeed!

I abandon that one in favor of the softer one. The same knee dance over here nets me a sliver of roasted pork. That's more like it.

More, bitch. Now. I jump again at the knee and speak more forcefully. A bigger piece. I do my best wolverine impression. I need more, more, more. I snap and swallow until I get another gobbet of bread. I am NOT pleased. I require MEAT. I bare my teeth and LEAP upward, toward the bare throat; I latch on. I am CARnivore. No more hideous hats. Ever. As the first iron-sweet pungency hits my ravening tongue, it all fades...

"Paaaaaacoooooo. Hewwo, sweetums. Oh Henry, look how cute he is in his little basket, twitching those itty-bitty legs, dreaming like a widDLE ANgel. Come here, mama's wittle man, time for walkeeeeees."

As the strap snaps across my chin I savor – and cling to – the last moments in that not-here place . . .

* * *

Mitchell? Mitchell! . . . MIIITCHELLLL!!!

Oops. Ticked off Mom again. She hates it when I get to daydreaming and lose track of time. I'm supposed to rake the leaves and watch Baby while she takes Josh to the orthodontist. Or is it the ENT, again? It's always something with him.

I can't see anything out of the one small window cut in the side of the box that has been my fort and refuge. I lean forward and carefully lift up the side. I see the stout leg of our oak dining room table and the slimmer ones of my mother. I hear impatient drumming on the tabletop. I set the box down and lean the other way, lift the opposite side. I see Baby's fat little arms and one beady blue eye. She breaks into squeals of laughter. Busted.

I lean the box on my head and pull my little sister into my lap to look adorable as Mom bends down to make her point. Our eyes meet and the frown she was trying to hold completely cracks up. She bursts out laughing because I am sitting under the table with the edge of a box on my head and a baby on my legs, which end in Halloween clown shoes. I'm wearing the nose and the little flowered hat, too. Gotta be prepared.

"Watch Ella," she says, still laughing. "I'll call if we're going to be back after 5." She tweaks Baby's pudgy toes. "Bye bye, punkin."

I am leaning forward to look at Baby's face so I see the start of a lip quiver. I circle her chubby arms with my hands and say, "Wave to Mama!" I wave the hands and then smack myself in the rubber nose with one. Baby starts squealing again and Mom leaves calling, "Thanks, Tige. See you soon. Joshua! Downstairs now!" I hear the thumping on the stairs and then the murmur of some futile back-chat. Josh should know better than to think he'll get away with anything with Mom. The front door closes and I am alone with Baby and my thoughts.

Afternoon sunlight filters through the windows, baking warm parallelograms onto the hardwood floor. I scooch out from under the table and sit in one with Baby, who has taken off my nose and is chewing on it. We just learned parallelograms. And rhomboids. I like the word and use it to torture Josh, who thinks it's some kind of big kid swearing. Mom just rolls her eyes.

We sit in the sun for a while, until Baby gets sleepy and starts to nod off. I lift her as carefully as I can and carry her upstairs for her nap. I set her in the crib, crank up the little wind-up mobile that plays goofy baby songs and tiptoe out. On the way out the door I turn on the baby monitor. I take the speaker from the kitchen put it on the front porch and turn the volume up.

I get the rake from the shed and start on the leaves. The air is cool and the sun is bright – I wouldn't tell Josh this, but I like doing it. I don't realize I'm still wearing the hat and clown shoes until Mrs. Pinsky comes by with her dog. She is pushing a shopping cart; the dog is tiptoeing on its hind legs, pushing a tiny version of an identical cart. I do a double take. So do they. The dog's hat is not much different from mine. As they stare I feel my face redden and I start to stammer something. The baby monitor squawks and I am saved from explanation.

Upstairs I pick up Ella, red-faced and pouty, and her favorite blanket, and we settle into the rocking chair in the corner. She leans against me, sucking her thumb and sniffling a little. She rubs the ribbon edge of the blanket against her cheek and I rock in the chair until she falls asleep again. Even though the leaves are only half-done, I am not far behind her.

* * *

I rub my hands over my face and look around the room as if I have never seen it before. In truth I have not "seen" anything for hours. The only reason I have put down my pen is that it is out of ink. Also the cat has started to gently knead his paws on my leg in an attempt to prod me into the realization that it is long past suppertime, at least for him. If I do not feed him, he will proceed to more persuasive methods.

It is not easy to rise. My legs and back are stiff. Splaying my fingers out from their grip on the pen sends tiny streaks of fire screaming toward my elbow. All thought, all energy has gone into the words. The rest is flat. A cardboard world compared to what stares at me from the page. My eyes see what is in front of me in sepia tones. The everyday is no longer believable.

I feed the cat.

I stand at the sink while coffee brews, staring at the few tiny lights across the pond. I absently munch a few crackers. They are dry, a bare sustenance. I don't notice. My thoughts feed in that other space. They grow fat, bursting forward.

I don't remember pouring the coffee, dragging a throw off the couch to wrap my legs, grabbing something to write with from the desk. (I will realize much later it was a laundry marker.) I see only the thick stack of paper on the table, invitation to worlds without end. I flatten one hand against the oak, take a deep breath, and accept.

Epilogue

I write this late at night with hands dusted in flour. I have been baking. Bread – the stuff of life. I am surrounded by essential simplicities: The alchemy of flour and sugar and yeast. The heady perfume that will fill the kitchen shortly. The jockeying of the cats for a favored spot in my lap. The slip of ice against the side of a glass.

I write of worlds within worlds. I call the piece "Kachina". It finally occurs to me that this is odd. In my home – that place I came from, that knew me as a child – that's what we called those nested Russian dolls that come painted in lovely red filigree, layer upon layer, mama and daughter and daughter, until the baby is uncovered, at the heart, kept safe. I have no idea where this appellation came from, but it was the word we always used. There is Russian in my heritage, my great-grandmother spoke it. Family legend says that we spent so much time with my mother's grandparents, that when I first spoke, I did so with a Russian accent. So I never thought to question that "Kachina" was the right word.

This is a complete myth.

Kachina dolls are Hopi. They are sacred, representatives of the spirit world. They are not toys, are not layered, and bear no resemblance to the brightly painted Russian dolls. Kachina, in its real language, means "Bringer of Life".

The Russian dolls have a number of names. One of them is matryushka – little mothers. This is a delight. I have had the right idea, just from the wrong way around. I can live with that. What is "real" comes to us any number of ways. The trick is to see, to listen, to hear – and be grateful.

Carol Brodtrick is a writer whose work has appeared in literary and gardening magazines, newspapers, and newsletters. She is a Marshall graduate and enjoyed a career in Public Broadcasting before retiring to focus on writing for children and young adults. She has completed several courses for credit at the Institute for Children's Literature and attended the prestigious Chautauqua Conference for Children's Writers as a scholarship recipient. She is a member of the Society of Children's Book Writers and Illustrators and has recently completed a novel for young adults, which won an award at the 2008 West Virginia Writer's Conference. She is working on a mystery novel.

Journey To Where?

The reality of my husband's illness set in slowly, in distressing, sporadic trickles over years, always bumping against denial.

It was a journey that began in his mid-sixties. He began forgetting names, places, and events. He became passive, a bit uncertain.

Natural, right? Memory loss happened as we grew older, and couldn't the chemicals he'd used in his work play their part in this pattern of forgetfulness and personality change?

It's what I wanted to believe. It's what he did believe.

Even so, I wanted the assurance of a medical person.

That was not to be. His insistent refusal to see a doctor allowed all of us – me, our sons and daughters, his brother and sisters, our friends – to pretend. With no clinical diagnosis, we substituted our own. We blamed his employer for the use of chemicals such as Chlorothene in their plant. We embraced the reasoning that use of such chemicals might damage parts of the brain over a long period. Such acceptance gave us cause and effect and we could rationally explain his differences in behavior. None of us looked beyond that.

Still, it didn't stop the ground-in worry that wakes you at two in the morning. It didn't blind awareness to the fact that, over time, he'd lost weight, he'd stopped visiting his best buddy, and would sometimes, uncharacteristically, fly into a rage when unable to find a wrench or screwdriver, thinking a son, or neighbor (or wife), had borrowed and not returned it. That's when, with the help of some Internet research, I began labeling his problem "early dementia."

I hoped the journey would end there, that lots of B vitamins and memory support supplements would slow the problem indefinitely, but reality has a way of imploding any artificial premise and often it takes something simple. Just after this past New Year, my husband's brother stopped by to leave a packet of pictures he thought we'd like to have. The black and white photos were of a long ago day in June – our wedding. I watched my husband as he studied each in turn, seeing himself as he was all those years ago, a laughing twenty-six-year-old man, tall and muscular, his arms around me, the adoring new bride.

His expression softened and grew wistful. He looked through the pictures again and again. Pointing to one or another of his groomsmen, he'd say, "That's Harley (or Arden, or Skip). He's dead now, right?"

Finally, he put them gently on the counter, patting them, nodding his thanks to his brother.

Later that day I took the pictures downstairs to my office, expecting to add them to our box of family pictures. Instead, I placed them in single file on the desk and, looking through a magnifying glass, brought each into sharp focus. A door, locked for a long time, opened, and forty-five years disappeared. We were young and the day was golden; daisies and baby's breath filled the church, incense scented the air and the glow of candles threw a halo of light around the altar. The pews filled with smiling parents, family, and friends.

How certain I was as I slow-stepped my way to my smiling husband-to-be, blonde, blue-eyed, a gentle giant.

How I loved his sharp intelligence, easy laugh, teasing ways.

I remembered how he loved me.

I tried to remember when it was he left me, replaced by the stranger downstairs, puttering in his workshop. When did I really begin to notice his loss of focus, quick understanding, that ready smile? Five years ago? The signs were there that long ago . . . the forgetfulness, hesitation, confusion . . . The screaming voice inside my head forced the admission that his was a greater problem than mild dementia.

He stopped driving voluntarily. No one had to take his keys. He said, one day after coming home from a short trip to a local hardware store, "Think I'd better give it up."

"Why?" I asked. "What happened?"

"Well, I drove to the bottom of the hill and couldn't remember which way to turn. And when I did turn, I couldn't remember where I wanted to go, so I just drove until something looked familiar. Then I turned around and came home."

He drove a few times after that, and though I asked to go with him, he didn't want me to, insisting he didn't need a "babysitter." He hung up his keys for good three years ago, in late autumn, just before the cold rains began. He used the winter to work on projects in his workshop, staying home more, declining social invitations. Over the next few years, he made our home his world, rarely agreeing to dinner out, a visit to family, a walk up the street.

He resisted all our pleas to see a doctor, saying no doctor could give back what the chemicals had taken. When I made an appointment for him, thinking he'd go if it was scheduled, he said to me, "You can make all the appointments you want, but you can't make me go."

His frustration increased, as it took longer to figure how things went together. He swore when plumbing leaked or the mower wouldn't start or the refrigerator began chirping, because he was the fixit guy and, as he put it one day, "I can't remember how to fixit anymore." Yet, he'd try. Simple, one-hour tasks grew into full-day ones. Some problems he ignored.

When I hired a serviceman to check the furnace that wasn't working right, he yelled about spending money we didn't need to spend, and didn't speak to me for days. He couldn't stand seeing another person do what he'd been able to do for so many years. He fought with himself, one personality insisting he could still function as well as always, the other insisting he couldn't.

It made sense to keep household problems from him. Whatever I could fix myself, I did. Whatever our sons could take care of on the sly, they did. Some problems remained problems. I learned to lie about repairs. As his memory worsened and he couldn't remember how a problem got resolved, I often countered with, "It works fine. Don't you remember doing that?"

Sometimes it took black humor and understanding friends to cope with situations I couldn't control. Sharing stories helped. It let me know our family could get through whatever this journey brought, even with dimmed hope and shredded patience.

Selfishly, we wanted a doctor along; though we knew it would take a crisis to force my husband to agree to seek medical help.

It came in the spring in the form of severe hip pain. But he suffered for two months before agreeing to see a doctor. Tests showed arthritis in the spine. Other tests proved what we had come to suspect; he did have the dreaded "A" disease.

We know now Alzheimer's is a sneaky disease. It robs memory, self-assurance, awareness, but not all at once. It triggers flash anger and stubbornness. The progression is slow and it is devastating to watch someone you love watch himself lose himself.

I still don't understand how some days can seem normal; days when he appears to think clearly, remember accurately; how other days are like hitting a brick wall.

Today we move from plateau to plateau, enjoying the days he feels comfortable, the good days when he reads, remembers a lot, and is in little pain. We tolerate the days his mind seems stuck and he asks the same question a dozen times.

He does not know he has Alzheimer's. I believe he doesn't need to know.

New crises dot our journey. Some small, like adjusting medication so it gives a steady ease to the arthritis pain he'll always have. Some large, like stomach upsets, persistent diarrhea – rollercoaster side effects of Aricept, the highly touted medicine for Alzheimer's patients. It's said to slow the disease and I had hoped it would help my husband.

Brodtrick

Sometimes I cry, because I know the progression accelerates. I don't cry for us, his family who watch. I cry for him, because his essence keeps dribbling away and I can't stop it.

We take this journey in one-day increments, living the day, never thinking about tomorrow. For now, it's almost enough.

Marc Miller is a prose writer and a poet. He has a Bachelor of Arts degree in Chemistry from Vanderbilt University, and completed a year of post-graduate studies at West Virginia University. Marc is currently employed at Dutch Miller Chevrolet as an automobile salesman, and has been in the automobile business for thirty years. He has written several unpublished short stories and has recently completed a soon-to-be-published novel titled *A Season of Hope*.

One of the Best Days of My Life

After a long, hard week of selling cars and trucks at Dutch Miller Chevrolet-Hyundai, in Huntington, West Virginia, Saturday night had arrived. I finally settled into bed. My wife, Susan Miller, waltzed into the bedroom and announced her idea for a fund-raiser for The Child Development Academy at Marshall University.

"Let's have a Troy Brown Fantasy Football Camp for adults," she said.

How was I supposed to sleep after that?

From that moment, nearly two years transpired of weekly meetings at Francois' Bakery with Troy's wife, Kim, Jane Boylin from Camden Park, and several more committee members, before the idea came to fruition. As a result, on Saturday, March 31, 2007 I found myself, at seven o'clock in the morning in the Marshall Culinary Institute on Fourth Avenue, having breakfast with the twenty-eight players who had signed up for the camp, and half a dozen coaches.

I began preparing myself mentally to undergo the "combine" drills scheduled to take place at seven forty-five that morning. The combine drills consisted of the forty-yard dash, the vertical jump, the broad jump and the cone drill. The cone drill is an alternating sprint and stop drill between rubber pylons, to test your agility. These drills were similar to those performed in the NFL camps, and our performance would be the basis for each player's position in the draft selection. During breakfast I reassuringly told stories of my days as a high school quarterback to the other players around our table to try to calm my nerves. Perhaps I neglected to mention I'm fifty-nine.

Eventually I turned and recognized Troy Brown seated at a table behind me, cool and confident, dressed in his white warm-up decorated with the New England Patriots' insignia. I had seen Troy play at Marshall University and on television with the Patriots, so I was aware he played bigger than his almost six-foot stature, but what I didn't know was his smile later that day would light up the room. I also noticed the smooth, dark, almost adolescent features of his face. More importantly, I believe Troy is what an NFL player should be. In the sports world it is common knowledge that he took a salary cut to play last season, his fifteenth season for the same team. His fifteen seasons with the Patriots is something quite extraordinary in these days of free agency. Plus the fact he plays both offensive receiver, defensive back, and special teams with equal enthusiasm. Couple his salary considerations and his willingness to play any position on the field, and it indicates, at least to me, that he plays football for the love of the game. He is what I wanted to be, if I could have been talented enough to play professional football. I could imagine Troy sitting serenely in a locker room preparing for any one of the Patriots' three Super Bowl victories.

Several minutes later all six feet four of Chad Pennington walked through the door, dressed in green Bermuda shorts and a white polo shirt. His white baseball cap sat atop youthful blonde hair that curled in all directions from underneath it. Up close he appeared massive for a quarterback. His upper body was extremely well defined and exuded an aura of durability. I remembered Chad when he was red-shirted, after he had taken Marshall to the Division 1AA National Championship. How I admired him for the way he came back after his red-shirt year and took the team to the GMAC Bowl! He has progressed, both as an NFL player and a leader, to the point that this past season he was elected the NFL's Comeback Player of the Year for his performance with the New York Jets after shoulder surgery.

By comparison, I had not reacted nearly so well when I was red-shirted at Vanderbilt University many years before. In 1966 I was red-shirted as a quarterback when Vanderbilt recruited a Junior College transfer from California, Gary Davis, and I was moved to number four on the depth chart and eventually to middle guard. I became so discouraged that I joined the Marine Corps in the middle of spring practice the same year. Today at breakfast in the same room with both Troy Brown and Chad Pennington, I was convinced that I was in the presence of professional football greatness. I only hoped I could perform to their satisfaction.

After breakfast the players boarded fifteen passenger vans that transported us to the Joan C. Edwards Stadium parking lot, where we would debark for the new indoor weight facility. There we would receive instructions and warm-up for the combine drills. The indoor weight facility became the chosen site for the drills, as the morning rain had forced us indoors. As we entered the Shewey Athletic Building and proceeded down the main corridor, I was overwhelmed by the sight of the framed jerseys lining the walls. There was Chad's Jets' #10, Troy's Patriots' #80 and the third coach, Mike Bartrum's Eagles' #88. As I continued down the hall toward the weight room, the jerseys further reminded me that within minutes these NFL greats would be conducting simulated NFL combine drills. My heart was nearly beating out of my tee shirt and my rain-soaked slicker.

As I entered the facility, I was concerned with the ability of my left knee to support me in the forty-yard dash, the first event of the day. But in the presence of Chad, Troy and Mike, I was motivated to do whatever was asked of me, or collapse trying. Troy directed the players collectively through a series of stretching and warm-up drills along the rubberized running track adjacent to the weight stations. Suddenly, the moment came for which everyone had been waiting, the forty-yard dash for time.

I positioned myself third to run, as I didn't want my muscles to get cold. Chad stood at the far end of the track at the forty-yard marker, with a stopwatch in one hand and his other hand raised to indicate he was ready to time me. I started off low to the ground and pushed off hard. My knee held and I finished the dash to resounding applause. I wasn't sure if the players and coaches were applauding my time or merely the fact that I had finished. Frankly, I didn't care.

As I hit the padded wall and circled past Chad toward the other end of the track, he held out his cupped hand, which I immediately slapped.

"Good effort," he said as I passed. That was all the encouragement I needed to complete the remaining combine drills. Each individual event began and ended with applause. The enthusiasm generated by our coaches filled the facility. I felt like I was trying out for the NFL.

After the drills, coaches and players returned to the visitor's locker room in the Shewey building for the draft selection. The draft was the selection process that assigned players to either the green team, coached by Chad Pennington, or the white team, coached by Troy Brown and Mike Bartrum. I was drafted in the eighth round by the white team. To say that I was elated would be a serious understatement. Troy gathered the white team together in the locker room after the draft.

"Winning is in the mind," he said. "Don't eat too much lunch and make sure to drink plenty of water. The game is in three hours."

Everyone, players and coaches together, left the locker room to watch Marshall's "hoot and holler" drill. This drill was the climax of the first day of spring practice in pads for the Marshall University football team, because it is a chance for the players who haven't had "contact" since the end of last year's season to enjoy the first contact of the spring. It consists of three offensive linemen, a quarterback and a running back trying to run the ball into the end zone against two defensive linemen and a defensive back, The "hoot and holler" drill continued to fuel the fire of enthusiasm for the fantasy football game, which was to take place in less than two hours. Game time was approaching quickly.

After lunch we took the field to warm-up for an hour before the game. By some miracle the rain had stopped minutes into our practice session. On the field I met Mike Bartrum for the first time. Mike impressed me instantly with his rugged good looks and his quick smile. He was six five or so, square jawed, broad shouldered, and lean. I shook his hand and immediately felt his strength. I later learned he was elected to the 2005 all-pro team as a long snapper. Although I had seen him at the "hoot and holler" and had recognized him, I didn't meet him until he huddled the team at the forty-yard line. He and Troy asked if anyone could throw the football. I raised my hand so hard and fast I thought I pulled a muscle. I was allowed to practice at the quarterback position and completed the second ball I threw in practice. As the practice continued, however, I found myself underthrowing the receivers.

Troy came over to me and said, "Marc, you need to follow your throw all the way through until your body faces the receiver."

That was such great advice and I began throwing so well that Chad sent Aaron Ferguson and Dinero Marriott, green team assistant coaches, to spy on us. Scotty Archer, from Archer's Flowers, was my back-up, but because he was in his mid-twenties and could run, he became much more valuable as a receiver. Because I was older and relatively immobile, I became the starting quarterback, thank God!

We lost the coin toss, but the green team elected to defer possession until the second half. I should have realized at that moment we were playing against Chad Pennington, one of the best football minds in the NFL. We were playing "flag football," a game in which the players are dressed in only shorts, tee shirts, and sneakers. Belts with flags attached are worn around the players' waists. In order to simulate a tackle of an opposing player, the defensive player must remove the offensive player's belt. There is no tackling or blocking. The offense must advance the ball from the five to the fifty-yard line to score. We had worked out signals, cadence and an assortment of running and passing plays in the brief hour of practice before the game.

Mike and Troy sent in the first play. It was a hitch and go route designed to influence the defensive backs into thinking we were throwing short, then suddenly both receivers on both sides of the field break for the end zone along the sidelines. Scott Barber, an investment banker and Marshall University board member, was covered on the left, but Scottie Archer was wide open down the right sidelines. I launched a perfect spiral and Scottie caught the ball full stride; he floated into the end zone. Toriano Brown, a former Marshall defensive stand-out, caught the extra point in the end zone and in the first minute of the game we were ahead 7-0.

My God! Does it get any better than this?

"Damn, Miller can throw," Chad said from across the field.

Chad's green team also scored in the first quarter and tied the score 7-7. We scored again in the second quarter, as did the green team, and at half time the score was tied 13-13. For me to compete in a game I love to play, on a sunny Saturday, with players and coaches I admired, was thrilling.

On the sidelines during half time, Troy's sons, Sir'mon and SaanJay, and their friends brought us Gatorade and water. During half time I had an opportunity to chat with Dr. Gerald McKenny, the team doctor for both the green team and the white team, on the sidelines. He confided to me that he was considering playing next year. He informed me he had been a receiver at Morehouse College, and I promptly asked him if he had good hands. Can you imagine asking a surgeon if he has good hands?

In the second half Chad changed his defensive scheme to a cover three, a deep zone coverage, which virtually eliminated the deep passing lanes. I tried to force the ball into deep coverage, and was subsequently intercepted several times. Midway into the third quarter Lewis Green, President of Robinson Construction in Cannonsburg, Kentucky, and a green team linebacker, tackled one of our receivers to prevent him from gaining additional yardage. That play nearly caused a riot! There were so many penalty flags on the field I thought I was at White Way Laundry and Dry Cleaners. The "tackle," though illegal, demonstrated the green team's determination to win and could have been the turning point of the game. Our white team failed to score in the third quarter, but our defense also held the green team scoreless and the score remained 13-13 going into the fourth quarter. In the closing minutes of the fourth quarter, Daniel Afzileride, the green team's quarterback and the game's MVP, threw a touchdown pass to take the lead 19-13. With less than two minutes remaining, we had one last chance to score and I felt we could do it. On third down and long I completed a pass to Mike Patick, Marshall student and son of HIMG's Dr. David Patick. We had the ball first and goal. I was sacked in the backfield on the next play. We had one final play to score before the clock expired. Before I could get the pass off, however, my belt fell off. Whether a result of a defensive player's efforts or by accident, the fact that my belt fell to the ground signaled the end of the game.

As good sportsmen, players and coaches from both teams gathered in line at midfield and shook hands and hugged each other after what had been a very competitive and hard fought game. A few minutes later I sought out Mike Bartrum to thank him personally for the enthusiasm and passion he brought to the game.

"Mike, it was an honor to be on the same field with you," I said.

"Are you kidding, Marc?" he said. "I had a ball."

We hugged each other enthusiastically and he lifted me off the ground! I couldn't believe it. I weigh two hundred and fifty pounds, and he lifted me off the ground. It was that kind of day. Everyone won on that day – the coaches, players, fans, media, family members, but especially The Child Development Academy at Marshall University, for which the Troy Brown Fantasy Football Camp raised thousands of dollars for scholarships for pre-school children.

Paul Martin's short fiction has appeared in publications as diverse as *The Cosmic Unicorn* and *Dogwood Tales* and has won recognition from *Glimmer Train Stories* and West Virginia Writers, Inc. In 2001 he was awarded the Fellowship for Fiction from the West Virginia Division of Culture and History. He currently lives and writes in Huntington, WV, with his wife Debbie.

Lawrence Ferlinghetti in the Restroom

When facing an unfamiliar intersection, I have a tendency to go left. Maybe it's because I'm left-handed, but for some reason left seems to feel, well, right. More often than not it has been the better choice. It is because of that tendency that I met Lawrence Ferlinghetti last Friday in the restroom.

He was to give a reading that evening in Tippler Auditorium at my university, and I got there a little too early. I picked up a program from a mahogany table where a grad student I recognized was selling books of beat poetry. There was a display in the lobby of some of Ferlinghetti's drawings, but I don't know squat about art, so his sketches all looked like the same naked man and woman in a variety of improbable chiropractical positions. I tried amusing myself by comparing the man's genitalia from one picture to the next to see if it was indeed the same guy. It was so laughably inaccurate, though, it was tough to say. The model seemed inordinately proud of himself I thought.

I couldn't kill more time among the pictures without appearing to be a connoisseur or a pervert, so I went in search of a restroom. I only mildly needed to go, but I could at least walk confidently as if I had a purpose, a destination. A sign told me, told anybody really, the restrooms were downstairs. At the bottom of the steps, though, there were no further clues about which direction to go. I, of course, went left.

About halfway down the long, antiseptically institutional hallway, I saw a doorway marked "Men's Faculty Restroom." Ordinarily I would have been intimidated by such a sign – an undergraduate peeing where learned academicians pee? But there are no night classes on Fridays, so I thought what the heck, you only live once.

I pushed through the door; the light was on. It looked like the students' restrooms only smaller: black and white tiled floors, two white stalls, two porcelain wall-mounted urinals, a sink. I faced one of the urinals and unzipped.

"Is that you, Dr. Huffman?" a voice asked from a stall.

I flinched. I got pee on my left hand. "You scared me to death," I said over my shoulder. "No, it's me." I realized immediately how ridiculous that statement sounded and thought it best to simply zip both my pants and lips, walk back out the door, and retain my anonymity.

At the squeak of my sneakers on the blinding floor tiles, the stall spoke again. "Just a moment," it said in a thin baritone. The stall must be old.

"I'm sorry," I said. "I'm not in the right place; I'm not Dr. Huffman."

"That is irrelevant, now. I wonder if I might impose upon you for a moment." It was less a request than a command.

There was nothing in the stall's tone, however, that indicated anything indecent, but you can never be too sure these days. "I don't know. What do you want?"

"For God's sake, there's no need for paranoia. I just needed some toilet paper. I was going to get it myself until you came in. Could you just check the empty stall for some?" He sighed. At least I think it was a sigh. When he finally spoke again, the voice sounded weary, farther away. "I'm Lawrence Ferlinghetti."

The first thing that struck me was that I had never once announced my full name while sitting on the toilet. I might have said "it's me" or something, but I'm not really sure I've done even that. The second thing that struck me was that that was Lawrence Ferlinghetti on the other side of that gleaming white metal stall, and he had. I removed the roll from the empty stall and handed it over the connecting partition. A hand reached up, fingertips cupped as if they were plucking fruit, and accepted the paper.

"Thank you," the stall said flatly.

"Welcome."

71

Propriety should have demanded that I leave the restroom after handing him the paper, but I didn't. I stayed in the stall beside his and looked down at his shoes. I expected to see something unusual but perfectly appropriate for a beat poet, maybe vaguely Oriental, but they were wing tips. The waistband of the black slacks that crumpled around his ankles was lined in blue plaid. I think I may have said "oh."

"Yes?" Lawrence Ferlinghetti said.

I couldn't help myself; I giggled. "Nothing. I'm sorry; I didn't mean anything." It needs saying that I'm a big fan of Lawrence Ferlinghetti's. I was turned on to his work by my Uncle James, who was by no means old enough to be a beatnik, but old enough to be a hippie. He wasn't, though; he was a redneck, he said, and fought in Vietnam. When he came home, wild-hearted and angry (Agent Orange for breakfast, lunch, and dinner, he'd say), he found his way to San Francisco. He still didn't become a hippie; that movement wouldn't stand the test of time, he thought, it lacked a soul, but Ginsberg and Kerouac and Cassady and Ferlinghetti, now, they stood for what was real. "It's a gone world, little man; there may be no way to get it back, but if there is, it's in here," he told me and handed me the copy of *Coney Island of the Mind* he had bought at the City Lights Bookstore. He died of lung cancer the next year, not broke, but certainly disillusioned.

Of course, I couldn't tell the voice in the stall that was why I giggled, that "yes?" it had spoken as if it were addressing its butler or valet. The laugh had been as much Uncle James' as mine. Once the stall had pronounced itself Lawrence Ferlinghetti, I had expected it to marvel at the surreal predicament it had found itself in, without toilet paper in a claustrophobic stall in the basement of a nondescript college in West Virginia, or to howl at the thoughtless injustice of the world and its tiny jokes. But the voice was old and refined, without edge, possibly saving itself for other, bigger battles.

The door to my stall squeaked slightly when I opened it. Ferlinghetti spoke: "Are you coming to my reading tonight? Forced to, perhaps, by a pedantic English professor, maybe to get some extra credit? If so, I apologize in advance. No one should have to go if they don't want to. It's certainly not the ideal way to be introduced to a poetry you've never heard of and probably can't understand."

I wanted to recite some of his own lines, to tell him that I, too, "am waiting for my case to come up/and I am waiting/for a rebirth of wonder/and I am waiting for someone to really discover America." I wanted to know if he could remember that as well as I did, to see if those words still meant to him what they had meant to Uncle James and now to me. I had come to this reading because I wanted to; I wasn't even taking an English course this semester. "Yes, I'm here for the reading," was all I told him, though.

The movement in the stall indicated he would soon be finished. He flushed. "Thank you, young man, for the assistance. If you're around after the reading, if you're not rushing off to drink some beer with your friends once you've gotten the program to validate your attendance to your professor, I will sign something for you." He laughed. "Maybe a signed roll of toilet paper would be appropriate."

The truth is I had brought my copy of *Coney Island of the Mind* for that purpose. It nestled in my jacket pocket, the top inch of its yellowing cover peeking out like an old tooth. Uncle James would have thought it cool for me to get Lawrence Ferlinghetti's autograph.

"Yeah. That would be great, an honor," I said. "I'll see you then." The door of the Men's Faculty Restroom slowed itself pneumatically behind me and closed with a low thud, maybe a smaller thud after that. Water splashed behind it – Lawrence Ferlinghetti washing his hands, I suppose. I could have waited in the lobby to see him, but I had a picture of him on the back cover of my book. Instead of turning left into the auditorium when I got to the upstairs lobby, I walked outside and stood at the top step and looked at the rugged Appalachian foothills across the highway. It was dusk, and a cement-colored sky promised rain and spring simultaneously.

I decided I didn't need to hear Lawrence Ferlinghetti read his poetry. At his book signing, he would wonder which hillbilly had handed him toilet paper, but he wouldn't ask anyone if it were him. Maybe Uncle James would find that funny, too; or maybe he'd be pissed at me for not getting my book signed. Patting my jacket pocket and pushing my book deeper into it, I jogged to the car just as a streetlight sizzled on.

Sit.

Stay.

Read.

Good Dog.

www.ingramcontent.com/pod-product-compliance
Lightning Source LLC
Chambersburg PA
CBHW031858170626
46807CB00004B/1785